'I Feel Cheate
Remember H
Tha

Clint told Skye.

'You remember a lot more than I thought you did.'

'Help me remember the rest.' He spoke just above a whisper.

All Skye's senses were on overload. Logic said she should get out of there as fast as humanly possible. But she knew she wouldn't.

She wanted to help Clint remember. Help him remember by making love with him again...

Dear Reader,

Great holiday reading *is* Silhouette Desire®—but even if you're not going away this month, there's always July's scorching novels to make you feel better! Lounge in the garden or by the pool with our MAN OF THE MONTH, Bryan Willard, from Lass Small's *The Coffeepot Inn*—absolute bliss!

Follow Trenton Laroquette's search for the right woman in *The Bride Wore Tie-Dye* by Pamela Ingrahm, and don't miss Beverly Barton's *The Tender Trap*—where an unplanned pregnancy prompts an unexpected proposal!

Talented award-winning author Jennifer Greene has created another seductive story with the second of the Stanford Sisters in *Bachelor Mum*, and there's something a little bit different from Ashley Summers, *On Wings of Love*.

The Loneliest Cowboy is Pamela Macaluso's charming story where the hero meets up with an old flame he can't even remember, so he gets the surprise of his life when he hears her long-kept secret!

Enjoy!

The Editors

The Loneliest Cowboy

PAMELA MACALUSO

™ SILHOUETTE
Desire®

*Silhouette, Silhouette Desire and Colophon
are registered trademarks of Harlequin Books S.A.,
used under licence.*

*First published in Great Britain 1997
Silhouette Books, Eton House, 18-24 Paradise Road,
Richmond, Surrey TW9 1SR*

© Pamela Macaluso 1997

ISBN 0 373 76048 5

22-9707

*Printed and bound in Great Britain
by Mackays of Chatham PLC, Chatham*

PAMELA MACALUSO

wanted to be a writer from the moment she realized people actually wrote the wonderful stories that were read to her. Since she is extremely curious and has an overactive imagination, writing is the perfect career for her. Curiosity is a necessary part of 'research,' and flights of fantasy can be called 'plotting'—terms she prefers to 'nosy' and 'wool-gathering.'

While she loves movies, Pamela would choose a good book over any other form of entertainment. It sometimes takes a search party to get her out of a library or bookstore.

Other novels by Pamela Macaluso

Silhouette Desire®

*Hometown Wedding
*Dream Wedding
*Christmas Wedding

Just Married

For Tom Barnes.
Thanks for watching all those cowboy movies,
Grandpa.
And an extra thank-you for teaching me to watch out
for the cows!

One

―――

Clint Slade strolled into the Rocking W Coffee Shop in search of a caffeine rush. He got a rush, all right, of the testosterone kind. Walking down the center aisle of the restaurant, holding a tray and heading toward a couple in the far corner booth was the shapeliest thing he'd seen in denim and boot leather. The cowbell tied to the knob clanked as he closed the door.

The woman didn't look his way, or break stride. "I'll be right with you."

Take your time, honey.

Clint pushed his black cowboy hat farther back to give himself a better view. Watching her walk was a pleasure. He couldn't put his finger on what it was he found so appealing, but damn, he sure liked the way she moved.

Her blond hair was braided in a single plait that hung down her back. He imagined himself untwining it, could almost feel its silky texture slipping through his fingers...

He watched as she refilled the customers' glasses with iced tea. They were the only ones here, besides himself. In an hour, after the bar across the parking lot closed, the place would be packed with people grabbing an early breakfast before heading home to sleep off their night out. But at the moment, it was quiet.

The waitress turned in his direction. Blue...he hoped her eyes were blue.

At first, she was smiling. Then a look that might have been surprise, or fear, flashed across her face before her lips settled back into a polite smile. Once she had closed the distance between them, he forgot about the changes he'd noticed in her expression and stared into her blue eyes.

"Would you like a table, booth or a seat at the counter?"

What he'd like and what he was likely to get were two different things. He forced his mind away from the need that had been developing while he'd watched her and onto the need that had brought him into the coffee shop in the first place—his fatigue and the twenty miles left on his late-night drive home from San Antonio to the Diamond S Ranch.

"Just coffee to go."

She nodded, then walked behind the counter, treating him to another look at the sway of her hips. He'd bet she was dynamite on the dance floor...not to mention between the sheets.

Attractive or not, he admonished himself silently, he shouldn't be thinking about her that way. He had a strict rule about not sleeping with any woman who lived within a hundred miles of Harmony Ridge, Texas. He liked to keep his business interests, his personal life and the satisfying of his physical needs separate so they didn't interfere with each other—it was a lesson he'd learned the hard way.

"New to town?" he asked. He hadn't seen her working here before. Of course, he usually came in during the day. It had been years since he'd been part of the late-night breakfast crowd.

"Cream or sugar?" she asked, clearly not interested in making small talk.

"Black."

She snapped a lid on the disposable cup containing his coffee, turned and carried it to the cash register.

After paying, he said, "You never answered my question. Are you new to town?"

She kept her gaze on the coins she was placing into the cash register drawer. Maybe she was afraid of him. Or maybe she was shy.

Something twisted in his gut as he looked at her. A sudden primal urge galloped through him. He wanted to take her in his arms, hold her, kiss her, sling her over his shoulder and carry her off.

Before he lost control and followed through, she looked up at him and said, "I...um...I grew up here, but I've been away for a while."

Clint studied her more closely, trying to put a name to her face. He didn't remember her. How could he have missed those baby blues and those feminine curves?

"Welcome home, then. Maybe once you're settled in, we could take in a movie." Okay, he thought, so it went against his rule, but what kind of self-respecting rule didn't have at least one exception?

"I haven't moved back permanently. I'm only here to help out while my father recovers in the hospital from his heart attack."

When he'd called this morning, Smokey Joe, the cook at the Diamond S, had mentioned Lou Williamson was in the hospital. "You're Lou's daughter?"

She nodded.

Clint knew that Lou and Marge Williamson, owners of the Rocking W Coffee Shop and the bar, had a whole passel of kids. He'd graduated from high school with their daughter Heather, played football on the same team as their sons, Beau and Chuck, and knew Alice because she'd been waitressing in the bar when he'd reached drinking age, but he didn't remember this woman. She looked about twenty-five or so.

"How's your dad doing?"

She shrugged. "Doc Beechem wants him moved to San Antonio for tests as soon as he can travel safely."

"If there's anything I can do to help, let me know. You can reach me at the Diamond S. The name's Clint Slade."

She looked him square in the eye. "I know who you are, Mr. Slade." Her voice had a coolness to it that puzzled him.

He'd never had any gripes with the Williamsons, so far as he could remember. In his younger days, he'd broken his share of furniture in brawls at the bar, but he'd always paid for the damages. Maybe he'd imagined the coolness, he decided. After all, he was overly tired and, with her father in the hospital, she had to be under a lot of stress.

"Other than your dad," he asked, "how are things with the rest of your family?"

"As well as can be expected." She glanced away, then back at him. "How's Teresa?"

Well, that explains her cool attitude.

She must think he's still married. How long had she been away from Harmony Ridge?

"She keeps cashing her alimony checks, so I figure she's fine."

"You're divorced?"

"Technically, five years ago. I was only married five months, so I feel more single than divorced."

Whoa, where had that come from? he wondered.

He hadn't consciously analyzed his feelings about his solo status before. Obviously his subconscious had worked out the matter. He didn't mind. What bothered him was that he'd never told anyone anything this personal until now, had never been tempted to. So why had he spilled his guts to a total stranger?

"Did you refuse my movie invitation because you thought I was still married?"

"No, I'm here to help pick up the slack at the coffee shop and bar until my dad is better or until they hire someone else," she told him. "I won't have time for socializing."

"Surely you'll have some time off?" he said.

"From work, yes, but there's all the household chores to take care of."

It seemed logical enough to be the truth, rather than a brush-off. "Well, then, give my best to your family." He tipped his hat, picked up his coffee and headed for the door.

He walked to his pickup, trying to convince himself that his body's reaction to Ms. Williamson and his personal revelation had been a by-product of too little sleep, too many hours behind the wheel and the endless litany of sappy love songs the country and western station had been playing on his truck radio.

Then again, he thought, maybe sometime after he'd caught up on his sleep, he'd drop by the coffee shop again. Just to see . . .

Skye Williamson tried to convince herself that she didn't care one bit that her daughter's father didn't know her from Adam. She watched until she could no longer see the taillights of Clint's pickup moving away along the Interstate 10. She took a deep breath and let it out slowly.

Clint Slade was as attractive as ever. Sure he looked six years older, but time had not detracted from his rugged good looks. And the familiar deep, smooth drawl hadn't changed a bit. It still sent shivers up her spine.

His fingers had brushed hers when he'd paid for the coffee. For a moment, she'd almost taken his large, work-roughened hand in hers. The casual touch had conjured up a crystal-clear memory of how he'd once roamed his hands intimately over her body—more intimately than any man before, or since.

His invitation to the movies didn't soften the disappointment that he hadn't recognized her. She'd been several years behind him in school, but there were fewer students at Harmony Ridge High than in big-city high schools. They'd passed each other plenty of times in the hall, but Clint had always had his eyes on whichever girl he'd had on his arm. Plus, Skye had to admit, she'd been a late bloomer. By the time she was turning guys' heads, Clint had practically been engaged to Teresa Donnelly, whose father owned the ranch next to the Diamond S. They'd formalized their engagement several months before Skye had left town.

Just then, the couple driving from Maine to California came to the register to pay their bill. She put on her brightest smile.

She'd spent six years dealing with the disappointment that in the dark and with as much as he'd had to drink, Clint hadn't realized who he'd made love to. But knowing he didn't even remember she existed hurt more than she would have guessed.

What did you expect? she asked herself. Violins? The swell of a full orchestra? Clint dropping to his knees to say he'd been looking for you for years, declaring his undying love?

It was an unlikely scenario, but she couldn't help imagining how good it would have felt.

The rest of the late-night crew started arriving, then the customers. As busy as things got, Skye couldn't banish the vision of Clint's dark brown eyes watching her from beneath the shadow of his Stetson. The shape of his eyes and the thick dark lashes were the same as her daughter's. But while Dawn's eyes sparkled with laughter and curiosity, Clint's flashed with sexual invitation backlit by confidence and a hefty dose of cynicism. It was a lethal combination.

When things finally slowed at the coffee shop, the regular staff voted unanimously that Skye should go get some sleep. She was grateful, knowing Dawn would be up early. After saying her goodbyes, she stepped out into the parking lot. Most of the vehicles in the lot were closer to the coffee shop, but there were still a few parked near the bar. She had worked the three-to-eleven shift before she'd left town, the bar parking lot was usually packed when she got off.

Her thoughts drifted back to one particular night. That night, she'd just gotten off work and was on her way home. She heard two voices having what sounded like an argument. The couple was moving in her direction and soon she recognized Clint Slade and Teresa Donnelly. The two had been an item for several months. Skye had assumed they were already lovers, but apparently not. From the sound of things, they weren't likely to be unless Clint came through with a wedding ring.

Clint had a reputation for getting any girl he wanted, and Skye assumed Teresa's refusal was a major blow to his ego. When Teresa stormed off in her car, Skye found herself feeling sorry for him. She walked over to Clint and invited him to the Rocking W for a cup of coffee.

"Coffee?" He looked at her as though she'd suggested a cup of rattlesnake venom. "You want me to drink coffee? That's just what I need! Then I can be wide-awake, drunk *and* horny as hell."

"I take it that's a no."

"Hey, one point for you, sugar."

Skye turned and started walking away, sorry she'd even bothered trying to help.

Sure, Skye, she'd thought, as if your main concern was to be helpful…it couldn't have anything to do with this being your one big chance to get Clint Slade to notice you're alive.

"Where in blazes is my truck?"

Clint's question wasn't directed at her in particular, but since she was the only person within earshot, she answered. "Probably right where you left it." She kept walking.

"Sugar, help me find my truck."

She'd helped him find his truck, all right. At that point, she should have walked away, but he'd offered her a kiss as a reward. Young, naive and in awe of the sexy cowboy—how could she resist?

The arrival of an eighteen-wheeler snapped Skye's thoughts back to the present. She finished crossing the parking lot, then the graveled road to her parents' home. After entering the house as quietly as possible, she tiptoed past the living room where her aunt and uncle were asleep on the foldout couch. Her mother's brother and his wife had driven over from El Paso to help out while her father was in the hospital. Skye continued up the stairs to the room she had shared with her two older sisters while growing up.

The room was lit by a soft night-light. In one of the bottom bunks, Dawn lay curled on her side, one hand resting under her cheek, the other holding on to a much-loved, stuffed Snoopy. Leaning over, Skye placed a gentle kiss on Dawn's forehead and tucked the blankets snugly around her.

My baby... my little girl... my daughter.

A surge of possessiveness spread through her. Despite the similarity in their coloring and their eyes, Skye rarely thought of Clint when she looked at Dawn. Other than that one night six years ago, he hadn't been part of their lives. But after seeing Clint Slade tonight, she couldn't help thinking about him.

Dawn's dark hair against the white pillowcase was a visual reminder that although Skye had been solely responsible for taking care of their child up to this point,

Clint had provided half the genetic material that had created Dawn.

A dull ache began to throb behind Skye's temples.

I can't think about this now. I have to get some sleep so I can be rested to help out tomorrow, and a splitting headache won't make it any easier.

She changed into her nightgown and climbed into the bottom bunk of the other bed. Although she was bone-tired, her mind was busy reliving Clint's visit to the coffee shop.

Terrific, Skye, start mooning over Clint Slade again. Nothing like asking for a bushel of trouble.

In an attempt to settle her thoughts, she looked around the familiar room. The two sets of bunk beds, nightstands and mirrored dresser were in pretty good shape considering they'd been hand-me-downs way back when. She looked across the room where Dawn was sleeping peacefully, completely oblivious to the turmoil her mother was going through.

The last time Skye had slept in this room, Dawn had been only a slight curve of her belly.

There wouldn't be any tranquillity thinking along those lines, either. It was going to be a long night.

Clint shot into a sitting position. The bed covers were a tangled mess and the shout of "Wait! Don't leave me!" hung in the air. He covered his face with his hands, then clawed his spread fingers through his hair.

Damn, he hadn't had that dream for almost a year now. The shadowy sights in the darkened cab of his pickup, the sounds, feel and taste of a woman having her sexual awakening in his arms. Tonight the vision had been as real as always.

The vision was so vivid that the first time he'd had the dream, he'd thought it was really happening. He'd been so sure that he and Teresa Donnelly had made love that he'd presented himself on her porch the next afternoon with an engagement ring in his pocket.

Not only because it seemed like the right thing to do after she'd surrendered her virginity to him, but because the power of the lovemaking had convinced him that he'd found the female who'd been made just for him. Since he'd found her, it would be senseless to look any further.

He'd walked around with his cowboy boots in the clouds and a perpetual smug smile on his face all through their engagement and up until he'd slid on top of his new wife, entered her and encountered a barrier that he was so sure he'd already passed through.

That's when he realized he'd been dreaming.

If he hadn't had such a hangover the morning he'd woken up in his truck, he might have checked for more definitive physical evidence than his jeans being open and pushed low on his hips. But the lovemaking had seemed so real, he hadn't even thought to question its authenticity.

Some of the ranch hands from the Diamond S confirmed that he'd left the bar with Teresa and hadn't come back in. They'd noticed his truck when they'd left, but since the windows were fogged, they'd figured

he and Teresa were making up after the fight that had
driven them outside.

He was a little surprised that Teresa had left him to
sleep it off in his truck, but he figured she'd tried to
wake him with no luck until she'd had to hightail it
home to meet her curfew. With his fuzzy memories of
that night, for all he knew, she might have left when he
was still awake.

The details weren't important. The bottom line was
that the best sex of his life had turned out to be a
dream....

Since he was awake and not likely to be able to fall
back to sleep, he got up, dressed and headed for the
mess hall. He ate alone in the ranch house most morn-
ings, but occasionally he joined the men.

"'Mornin', boss." Smokey Joe waved a spatula in
Clint's direction. No one knew how old Joe was. He'd
had a head full of gray and a beard to match as far back
as Clint could remember.

Clint returned the greeting with a nod and took his
place at the end of the breakfast line. The other cowboys added a respectful echo of the cook's reception,
which Clint acknowledged.

It was a diverse group. Some had been working on the
Diamond S since before Clint was born. Others had
been with the outfit off and on over the years, drifting
in when the cattle and the open range called to them and
drifting out when the lure of the open road was louder.
Some of the men had been born and raised in Har-

mony Ridge, while others arrived from somewhere else on their way to who knew where.

Even though he knew most of them by name, an invisible wall stood between him and them. It had been there as long as he could remember. First, as a barrier between the workers and the boss's son. Now, between the workers and himself as boss.

It was important that he have their respect, but he paid a price for it. While their loyalty to him and the Diamond S was undeniable, none of them were likely to invite him to join in their after-hours pursuits. And he wasn't likely to tell any of them how he felt more single than divorced... he still couldn't get over how he'd blurted that out last night.

Once he'd had his breakfast, Clint took his steaming mug of hot coffee and went to sit across the table from foreman Luke Conner.

"'Mornin', Clint."

"Luke."

"The boys have about finished breakin' in the new horses."

"Good. I saw a few more this week in San Antonio. If I buy them, do you think they can be ready to ride in time for the fall roundup?"

"I don't see why not. June just started."

They talked until Luke finished his breakfast and set off to work. Clint drank the rest of his coffee, then took the opportunity to slip into the kitchen and talk to Smokey Joe about Ms. Williamson.

The cook at the Diamond S always seemed to be on top of all the news in Harmony Ridge and the neighboring ranches. He knew the lowdown, and always managed to have meals ready on time. Clint didn't know how the man found time to do both.

Joe didn't have much information on her younger years, but he knew her name was Skye, she'd graduated from Harmony Ridge High and had worked in the coffee shop. "She was a cute enough kid, a bit on the scrawny side, but from what I hear, she's grown up to be a real looker." Joe winked and clicked his dentures together.

"Any idea where she's been since leaving town?"

"Don't know where all she's been, but I hear she's workin' at a dude ranch, cookin' up grub for city slickers who want to play cowboy for a week."

Clint didn't think there were any dude ranches within a hundred miles of Harmony Ridge. So Skye must live farther than that.

Just who are you trying to fool, pal? he asked himself.

When it came to Skye Williamson, his one-hundred-mile rule was already history.

"Mommy?" The question was a tiny whisper in Skye's ear.

She opened her eyes and smiled at Dawn. "Good morning, angel. Did you have a good night?"

"I had trouble sleeping, Mommy. It's too noisy here."

Last night had been their first in Harmony Ridge. Although Skye's old room was on the far side of the parking lot from the bar, she knew the bass line of the country and western music and raised voices from the parking lot carried. Added to that was the noisy comings and goings from the twenty-four-hour coffee shop only a narrow, graveled road from her parents' home. Many nights Skye had drifted to sleep humming along with the rumble of an eighteen-wheeler's engine.

As a child, she'd never known anything else, but it was new to Dawn.

"I know it's noisy, but it's only for a little while."

"I want to go home before next bedtime."

Me, too! Skye wanted to say. "When Grandpa's all better we'll go home," she told her daughter.

It was too soon to know *if* her father would get "all better," but she didn't want to add that uncertainty to Dawn's task of settling in to her new surroundings. She would carry the burden herself, along with the worry that Clint and Dawn might accidently cross paths.

Of course, since Clint hadn't even recognized her last night, she was probably worrying needlessly. Even if he noticed a resemblance between himself and Dawn, he would most likely consider it a coincidence.

The rest of the day was filled with a number of odd jobs. Skye took her turn answering the phone and cleaning up around the house. She picked out a fresh set of clothes for her brother to drop off at the hospital for their mother. Mrs. Williamson said she wasn't leaving until her husband regained consciousness or was stabilized enough for the trip to San Antonio.

At bedtime, Skye settled next to Dawn with a battered copy of *The Cat In The Hat*. Halfway through the book, she let her voice drift off to a whisper, watching Dawn for any sign that the little girl was still awake.

She closed the book, set it on the nightstand, then carefully scooted off the bed. Hopefully, the night noises wouldn't bother Dawn tonight.

An hour later, Skye set off for the coffee shop. The minute her boots hit the asphalt parking lot, thoughts of Clint rushed to her mind. From the day Clint hit drinking age, it had been second nature for her to check the parking lot for his truck. She used to find it parked there several nights a week and always on Saturday night. Her heart would beat double time when she spotted it and she'd cross her fingers in hopes of catching a glimpse of him.

She'd been so young, in years as well as life experience. Her dates were few and far between, what with her work schedule and two big brothers who'd already established their reputations as watchdogs with Alice and Heather's dates. It was a miracle anyone had been brave enough to ask her out at all.

The bravery had only gone so far, though. None of her dates ever took her to the drive-in or any of the local "parking" sites.

Maybe if she'd experienced more than a few chaste good-night kisses on her front porch, she wouldn't have reacted so strongly to Clint's kiss.

No, that was just wishful thinking. She doubted if anything could have prepared her for Clint's kiss—or what had followed.

You really shouldn't think about this now.

Focusing her gaze on a direct path to the coffee shop, she ignored the parking lot and the memories it evoked. Once she reached work, she tried to keep total concentration on her job.

She was having a moderate degree of success until shortly after midnight the clank of the cowbell announced a new arrival. It was Clint Slade.

Two

Clint's assessing gaze pinned her to the spot. For an instant, she feared that somehow he'd realized she was the one who'd been in his pickup that long-ago night, but she knew it was impossible. He couldn't have figured it out, she told herself.

Slowly, his lips curved into a smile and he tipped his hat to her. " 'Evenin', Miss Skye."

He strolled through the restaurant and slid his long frame onto one of the stools across the counter from where she stood.

She didn't remember telling him her first name last night. He must have asked someone about her. A spark of joy flashed in her, but was quickly squelched by the voice of fear and reason.

Look what happened last time you let yourself soak up attention from Clint! This is no time to let your ego get you in trouble again.

Returning Clint's interest would be an absolute disaster. She could imagine him showing up at the house during the day and Dawn answering the door. What would she say? "Clint, meet your daughter, Dawn. And Dawn, honey, this is your daddy." She shuddered inwardly. The idea was too awful to think about.

"Coffee to go, again?" she asked as evenly as she could.

"No, I'll have it here. What kind of pie do you have tonight?"

He was here for coffee and pie? It was after midnight. Of course, he might have been at the bar. But he'd gone to the trouble of finding out her name—maybe he'd come in to see her.

Or maybe he's taken a real liking to Rocking W coffee.

"Apple, blueberry and pecan," she said, listing the choices for him.

Clint narrowed his eyes and shifted his bottom lip a fraction of an inch to one side. Skye's breath caught in her throat. She'd seen that expression countless times. Dawn often did the same thing when trying to make up her mind.

Oh, please, no.

A sinking feeling swept through her, and just as it had when she'd looked at her daughter sleeping last night, the knowledge that Dawn was only half hers tugged at her heart.

As close as she felt to Dawn, was it possible for her to truly know her daughter without knowing the man who'd set the whole process in motion? Suddenly, she felt a strong urgency to learn more about Clint, to discover other similarities between him and the child he'd helped create.

But on its heels was a stronger urgency. The need for her to be cautious in order to protect herself and her daughter.

"Is there a problem with pecan? I can make another choice."

Skye snapped to, realizing she must have missed Clint's first request while her mind had been elsewhere. "Pecan is fine. Is that what you'd like?"

He nodded. "Are you all right?"

Before she could answer, he continued, "That's not really a fair question, what with your dad in the hospital, and all. How's he doing?"

At least he attributed her rattled state to her father's condition. Only she knew that his presence was the cause of the emotional war raging inside her.

"He's still in a coma, but Doc Beechem says his vital signs are improving. Hopefully, they'll be able to move him to San Antonio later this week."

"Glad to hear it. How's everything else going around here?"

Skye served him his coffee and moved to the end of the counter to get the pie. "All right. Reverend Bartlett asked anyone available to help out and we've had a rush of people come in to apply for part-time jobs.''

Had he really come in to make sure all was well with them? A phone call would have gotten him the same information.

She set the pie in front of Clint. He smiled his thanks. Still torn between drawing closer to him and keeping as far as possible, she gave him only a token smile in return. She picked up the pot of freshly brewed coffee and went to offer refills to the other customers, making her escape from Clint's disturbing presence.

Clint took a sip of coffee and reached for his fork. Coming back to the coffee shop may have been a mistake. Instead of proving his theory that last night's reaction to Skye had been a fluke, tonight's visit had proved the opposite.

The minute he'd walked in and spotted her, he'd had that odd feeling again. It was a sexual feeling, only more primal. The urge to pursue Skye with some macho, me-Tarzan-you-Jane method of seduction.

He watched her. He didn't need to hear the words to know the male customers were flirting with her. And she was flirting right back, with a sassiness that was worlds away from the standoffishness she used with him.

Maybe she was one of those women who got tongue-tied around a man if she was interested in him. He'd met that kind before. They took extra patience, but were usually worth the effort.

You should be so lucky this time, pal...

Most likely there was another reason. He mulled over a number of possibilities, but the one that seemed to make the most sense was that she wanted something from him. From past experience, the two things women seemed to want from him most often were sex and money.

Skye might be trying to work up the courage to ask for a loan of a large amount of cash, something to help the Williamson family stay afloat through Lou's illness and the medical bills that would follow.

Yeah, that had to be it, the reason she'd gotten that strange faraway look of yearning in her eyes. She'd probably been seeing a large, flashing dollar sign on his forehead.

Once she worked up the courage, he'd be getting the full force of her persuasive charms aimed in his direction. He'd play along with her, maybe even loan her the money. But everything would be on his terms, not hers.

He turned his attention to the pie, stabbing it with more force than necessary.

Skye had put off the inevitable for as long as possible, but finally she stepped behind the counter and headed toward Clint.

"Refill on coffee, Mr. Slade?"

Slowly, he raised his gaze to hers, moving it straight up her body starting from her waist. She froze like a deer caught in the glare of headlights. She'd seen that heated look in his eyes before. Not in bright fluorescent lighting, but in the pale glow from a rising moon and dim streaks from a parking-lot light.

Other memories teased her nerve endings. The taste and feel of his mouth, the sensation of his hands touching her and the exotic male textures and contours she'd discovered when she'd given in to his urging that she touch him in return. And as things had progressed, the uncontrollable way the force of his desire had sparked hers.

The fire in his eyes burned brighter. Then he blinked and that fast the flames went out. ''No, thanks. I need to be getting home.''

Had he only come in for coffee and pie, after all?

He stood and reached into his back pocket, pulling out his wallet. Skye tried not to let her gaze drift downward, but lost the battle. Did he still wear white briefs beneath the well-worn denim?

She felt the heat of a blush rush to her cheeks. Shifting her focus to the money in his hand, she asked, ''How was your pie?''

''Great, as usual.''

She stepped to the cash register, rang up his order, made change and wished him a good evening without looking him in the eye again.

Clint had the dream again in the early hours of the next morning. This time, he got up and headed for the stables.

''How ya doin', Zeus?'' He rubbed the black stallion's nose. ''Ready for a nice, long ride?''

Clint was. After two nights with a rude awakening from his dream, he needed the healing calm he got from being on his land. He saddled up, mounted and set off into the crisp morning.

From the first time he'd ventured out alone on the Diamond S, he'd felt a deep, almost spiritual, bond with the diverse territory that made up the ranch—the acres and acres of land scarred by arroyos, the rolling hills, deep ravines and rugged rockiness of buttes and mountains. Although they looked barren from a distance, hidden away in the westernmost mountain range were lush meadows abundant with wildlife.

This land filled a need deep within him. A need he sensed other people filled for each other. He got along well enough with people. Men respected him. Women were hot for him. But there wasn't anyone he considered a friend—someone he could really let down his guard with. Someone he could tell things to, like that bit about feeling single he'd babbled out to Skye the other night.

He must have been more tired than he'd thought, to have admitted something so personal to a complete stranger. The way his libido had reared up like a teenager's should have tipped him off that he wasn't in a state of absolute control.

Of course, he hadn't been as tired last night and she'd still pushed his hormones into overdrive. At least he hadn't dropped any more personal information.

Zeus came to a stop when they reached a fork in the trail, waiting for a signal telling him which way to go.

Clint decided to take the route along Harmony Creek to reach the herd. It wasn't a necessity that he check on them. The herd and the water were regularly monitored by plane or helicopter. In fact, much of the daily work on the ranch was done with the latest modern trappings, but when it came time for the spring and fall roundups the brunt of the workload fell on the cowboys and their horses.

There was something comforting in the knowledge they were following age-old traditions his great-grandfather had started.

He wondered about future generations of Slades. How would ranching be for them? More important, if he continued as he was, would there be future generations of Slades?

Skye woke to sunshine and the aroma of coffee. The first thing she saw was Dawn setting a ceramic mug on the nightstand. Skye scooted into a sitting position and caught her daughter as she bounced onto the side of the bed.

"Thanks, sweetie. Is Auntie Anna up?"

"Auntie Anna and Uncle Richard left for work already. Uncle Chuck made the coffee and carried it up the stairs for me. But I got to give it to you *mineself!*"

After another hug and thank-you for Dawn, Skye flew off the bed and across the room into the arms of the tall, handsome blond man standing patiently in the doorway. He had a deeper tan than she'd ever seen him with, but otherwise looked much the same...older, but the same.

Sister and brother said their hellos and commented on the changes six years had made.

"So, sis, both the black sheep have returned."

Her sister Heather had told her how several years after Skye had left, their brother, Chuck, had taken off to join the rodeo circuit.

"When did you get here?" Skye asked.

"About an hour ago." He gave her another heartfelt hug. "They tracked me through the Rodeo Cowboy's Association, but how did they manage to find you?"

"I have a friend who drives a rig," she told him. Gracie, the same friend who had given her a lift out of town when she'd left Harmony Ridge. "The truckers were talking about Dad's heart attack on the CB. I called to get an update and Beau suggested I come home."

Chuck's smile faded and his eyebrows pulled together in a frown. "So, how is the old man?"

"He's doing better. Mom's been the only one allowed to see him, so far."

"When the time does come for us to visit, I'll go with you."

"I'd like that." She nibbled on her bottom lip. "I'm a little nervous."

"You and me both." He hugged her tightly to him and patted her back. "We'll get through it together."

"Safety in numbers?"

"Hey, it's not like he can ground us, dock our allowances or make us peel potatoes."

"Mommy." Dawn tugged on Skye's nightgown. "Why's Granpa going to ground you and Uncle Chuck? Did you do something bad?"

Skye fought the urge to chuckle, then the urge to cry. Dawn's questions were so simple, so direct—Skye remembered when she'd looked at life that way, too. Before adult choices and emotions had complicated things.

Chuck reached down and tweaked Dawn's nose. "Your grandpa wanted me to stay in Harmony Ridge and work for him and I wanted to be in the rodeo."

"What about you, Mommy?"

Skye felt her heart in the pit of her stomach. She'd always answered Dawn's questions honestly but limited the details to keep things appropriate to her age. No way could she tell her little girl how the falling-out with her father had been because Skye had refused to divulge the name of her baby's father. Lou Williamson would have forced Clint to marry her, engaged to someone else or not.

It would have been a classic shotgun wedding. What sort of start was that for a marriage? Especially when she knew the groom was madly in love with another woman. She couldn't have faced it if each time they made love, he'd called out Teresa's name. Once had been bad enough.

"Grandpa and I had a disagreement," she said succinctly.

Dawn looked intently from one to the other of them. "I don't know if I want to meet *Granpa.*"

"Remember what we talked about? How you might not get to see Grandpa if he's too sick? So let's not worry about it right now, okay?"

"Okay."

"Who's ready for breakfast?" Chuck asked.

After breakfast, Dawn asked to watch the video of *Sleeping Beauty.* Skye expected Chuck would watch it with her, but he followed her into the kitchen. With a glance to the living room, he swung the kitchen door closed. The serious look on his face worried her.

"Is something wrong, Chuck?"

"No, I just don't want Dawn to overhear our conversation." He came to stand several steps from her. "Clint Slade is Dawn's daddy, isn't he?"

Chuck's question made Skye's stomach churn. "What makes you say that?"

"Her hair and eyes."

Skye laughed, trying to make light of the subject, while the knot in her stomach tightened even more. "Clint's not the only man in these parts with dark hair and brown eyes. Take into account the number of truck drivers who pass through and the odds decrease that much more."

"It's not just the coloring. After you ran away, Heather mentioned something about you having a crush on him."

If Heather knew about her crush on Clint, and Chuck had noticed the similarities between Dawn and the little girl's father, did the rest of the family know? Were they all speculating behind her back?

"Chuck, you're my brother, I love you, but this isn't any of your business."

"Is he giving you enough?"

"Enough?"

"Child support."

"Well . . ."

Chuck's eyes narrowed, the muscles along his jaw tightened and his hands clenched into fists. "Does he need some encouragement to pay his fair share? 'Cause I'll give it to him. Just say the word."

Skye crossed her arms over her chest, rubbing her elbows. "It's not as cut-and-dried as you make it sound."

"Why? Did he give you a lump sum up front and expect you to make it last for eighteen years?" Chuck started to get a wild look in his eyes. "Is it Clint, Skye? Tell me or I'll light into him until he owns up to it."

"That's not going to accomplish anything."

"Don't go giving me one of your little peacemaker talks!"

"It's not a peacemaker talk. It won't accomplish anything because Clint doesn't know about Dawn."

Chuck looked stunned, just short of horrified. "Doesn't know what about Dawn?"

"He doesn't know she exists."

Now he did look horrified. "You never told him you were pregnant?"

"By the time I found out, he was engaged to Teresa Donnelly."

Chuck swore beneath his breath. "So, he was out sowing the last of his wild oats and you ended up paying the price?"

Skye shrugged. Clint hadn't been deliberately sowing wild oats, but the description fit enough that she let it ride.

"You should have told him."

She squared her shoulders and raised her chin a notch. "Excuse me?"

"He had a right to know. He's her father, for crying out loud."

"I know guys have this whole male-stick-together thing going, but I'm your sister. You're supposed to be on my side."

Chuck planted his hands on his hips. "I'm not taking sides. I'm just saying a guy has the right to know when he's about to become a father."

"The talk shows are full of guests with cries for father's rights, but check around. Do a little impromptu poll at the Rocking W Bar tonight. You'll find a lot of men would rather not be bothered with news of an unplanned pregnancy."

"I sure as hell would want to know."

"I said *a lot* of men wouldn't want to know. I didn't say *all* men."

"Okay, so what gave you the right to make the choice for Clint?"

The fact that Clint didn't know he'd made love to her—that he thought he'd been making love to Teresa.

"I didn't sit down and consciously make the choice for him. I just did what I thought was best for me and my baby."

He took a deep breath, held it, then let it out with a rush. "What's done is done. The problem now is deciding when and how to tell him."

Skye couldn't believe her ears. "Tell him? I'm not going to tell him."

"He has the right to know."

"That's debatable."

"What about Dawn's right to know her father and her paternal heritage?"

Pain gripped her middle, the same stab she got every time Dawn mentioned "her daddy." Dawn knew her father was alive and a cowboy on a Texas spread. That information had kept her happy till now, but Skye knew someday she would ask for more. She hadn't decided what she would do when that day came.

"Obviously we're not going to agree on this," she said. "Let's just drop it, okay?" She gathered a handful of plates, glasses and silverware from the table and carried them to the sink.

"Someday Dawn's going to want to know more about her father," Chuck said. "What will you do then?"

"That's my problem, isn't it?"

"Skye, I want to help."

"The subject is closed!"

They didn't talk anymore about it, but the question of Clint's right to know about Dawn haunted Skye the rest of the day.

Almost as though her thought waves had reached out, lassoed and reeled him in, Clint was waiting for her when she went to work that night.

As she crossed the dark parking lot, the silhouette of a man separated from the shadows of the building and moved purposefully toward her. She recognized Clint's walk before he was close enough for her to recognize his features.

She came to a stop several yards from him.

"Hello, Skye."

"Clint." He had an unreadable look on his face. Surely Chuck wouldn't have gone to Clint behind her back and told him about Dawn. "A-are you here for coffee and pie again?"

Clint continued walking until the distance between them had shrunk to feet. "No, I stopped by to have a few words with you."

Chuck had told him! Now what?

"How's your father doing?"

"As well as can be expected." If he knew about Dawn, he was playing mind games with her. On the other hand, maybe Chuck hadn't spilled the beans.

Clint ran his hand over the back of his neck. "I've been wondering why we never met until a few days ago."

"We went to the same schools and the same church," she said. "I knew who you were."

"How did I miss you?" He took a step closer, reaching out to caress her cheek. "Are you working tonight?"

"Yes. Thanks for reminding me." She started to step past him.

Clint stretched an arm across her path, curving it around her waist when her momentum moved her against it. "Whoa, honey, not so fast."

Skye froze, torn between the urge to run away from him and the urge to curl the rest of the way into his arms. She remembered well ... too well ... the feel of being enclosed in his warm, powerful embrace. "I ... I'm due at work."

"How 'bout if I buy you a cup of coffee when you get off? Or we could go for a drive if you need some time away from the house."

"No, thanks. I'm training some of the new employees tonight, won't be getting off until late."

Skye slowly backed away from him until she came up against cold metal. From the height of the bumper, she assumed it was someone's pickup or four-by-four. Clint moved in so close, their bodies were almost touching.

He removed his Stetson, setting it on the hood, then placed his hands on either side of her. "Can I see you tomorrow then?"

"I have things to do."

Like take care of our daughter for starters, she thought.

"So do I, but I'll make time. I want us to spend time together, get to know each other."

Skye wanted to scream. Why couldn't he have said these words to her six years ago? Then she would have wanted to shout for joy. Now she wanted to shout out her frustration.

"I'm not going to be here that long."

"We're living in the age of phones and cars, darlin'. Your leaving doesn't mean we can't stay in touch or see each other again."

Raising one hand, he threaded his fingers through her hair, resting his warm palm against her cheek. With his thumb he tilted her chin up. He started to lower his head toward her.

"Hold on. What are you up to?"

Clint straightened. "I'm doing something I've wanted to do from the moment I set eyes on you."

Skye had to clear her throat to get her voice to work. "And what is that?"

"I'm going to kiss you."

Three

―――――

"**I** don't think that's such a good idea," Skye said. She *knew* it wasn't a good idea, but a flutter of anticipation stirred inside her nevertheless.

"I think it's the best idea since barbed wire."

She started to laugh, but the sound was trapped as Clint leaned down and placed his lips against hers. Floodgates burst open. For five years she'd been wrapped up in her role as Dawn's mother. In half a heartbeat of Clint starting to kiss her, she awakened to the forgotten fact that she was also a woman. A woman extraordinarily physically attracted to the man kissing her.

Skye knew she should slip away and put distance between them. Instead, she slid her arms around his neck and kissed him back. Clint moved closer until he was thrust tightly against her. A need grew within her and she remembered the night that had changed her life forever. She recalled the passion his touch had ignited, the burning desire that had driven her to make love with Clint.

With a soft sigh, she parted her lips. Clint slipped his tongue between them, probing, tasting, inciting more and more memories in Skye. What was it about the way this man kissed her, held her, touched her, that gave him the power to affect her so deeply?

She was six years older, six years wiser—he shouldn't be able to make her knees so weak, to make her melt against him.

Her only consolation was that the desire wasn't one-sided, the proof of his arousal pressed hard between them. Instinctively, she shifted her hips, rocking against him. He moved one arm to the small of her back, encouraging her to continue the subtle movement. He slid his other hand up to curve gently around her breast. Skye felt her nipple pull tight, then push forward, pressing against the fabric of her bra and blouse. Her reaction didn't go unnoticed. Clint moved his palm seductively over the area, intensifying the sensation.

The rumble of an engine and the harsh glare of headlights sweeping across them were an abrupt intrusion to their steamy kiss. With a honk, the car was gone as quickly as it had appeared, but the mood was shattered.

Clint moved back a step. The sound of them trying to catch their breaths was the only indication they'd been doing anything more than talking.

"I need to get to work," she said hoarsely.

"Are we on for tomorrow? Just pick a time and I'll be here."

Skye shook her head. "No. Long-distance relationships are possible, but I don't think we should start one."

"You're going to ignore what just happened?"

"We kissed each other. That's all that happened."

"And steers have udders!"

"Okay, so it was a very..." Hot, passionate, sexy? "A very good kiss, but still just a kiss. I've had a rough couple of days, I'm tired, stressed-out, and you've obviously had a lot of practice at this kind of thing."

"Stress and my reputed expertise had nothing to do with what was happening between us." He stepped forward, grabbed his hat from the hood of the car and put it on. "There was more to it than that. Now, if you plan on working tonight, you'd better get going before I decide to kiss you again."

Skye didn't need to be told twice. She expected him to follow her into the coffee shop. Instead, she heard the slam of a door and an engine roaring to life.

Clint woke up in pain. Carefully, he rolled from his stomach to his side. It relieved the external pressure from parts of his anatomy, but did nothing to relieve the internal pressure causing his arousal.

That damned dream again!

People spoke of a second childhood, maybe he was suffering from a second round of adolescence. The hell of it was that teenage boys only needed privacy and a confiscated magazine to find relief.

He closed his eyes, pretending he had a chance of falling asleep. Instead of dwelling on the dream, his mind chose to torture him with memories of kissing Skye last night.

Without a doubt, it was the most explosive first kiss he'd ever been part of. There was usually a tentativeness, a testing at the beginning of a kiss...especially a first kiss. Skye had gone off like dynamite. Once again he wondered if she had some kind of hidden agenda, something she wanted from him.

But she hadn't been the one waiting for him to come along in the parking lot...

True, but the way she'd returned his kiss might have been her way of taking advantage of the situation and trying to use it to further her own plans. But she hadn't made any move to follow up on the kiss. Not even a promise of more to come. In fact, she'd looked as surprised as he'd felt. Of course that might be part of her game, reeling him in slow.

He would be wise to see they didn't cross paths again.

Go ahead, be wise, his libido taunted him. *And unless you want to wake up in pain again, you'd better stop sleeping on your stomach.*

"Mommy, you're hugging too tight." Dawn's sentence ended with a squeak.

Skye loosened her hold and tucked her daughter's sleep-tousled hair behind the little girl's ears. "Sorry. How'd you sleep last night?"

"Okay." Dawn scooted out of Skye's arms, off the bed and over to the window. "Are the cowboys around here real cowboys like my daddy or pretend cowboys like the ones who visit our ranch?"

Usually, Skye would remind Dawn that the Bar K Dude Ranch wasn't theirs, it was only where Skye worked. But with Dawn bringing up Clint after Skye had spent most of yesterday thinking about him and the rest of it thinking about the kiss they'd shared, she decided to let the inaccuracy pass.

Skye sent up a silent prayer that after getting a short simple answer, Dawn would drop the subject of Clint. "Most of them are real cowboys."

"Do any of them know my daddy?"

A lot of them work for your daddy. The words flashed into her mind. She bit on her tongue to keep them from slipping out.

"I think so."

"Could I maybe get to meet him, like I'm maybe going to meet Granpa?"

Skye took a deep breath and grabbed for the small loophole Dawn had opened for her. "That reminds me...Grandma called last night at the coffee shop. Grandpa is awake now and they're going to fly him to San Antonio this afternoon. Grandma will be coming home sometime this morning and she's looking forward to meeting you.''

"Granpa, too?''

"No, he's going to fly straight from one hospital to the other in a helicopter." Skye got out of bed, holding her hand toward Dawn. "How 'bout if we surprise Grandma with a batch of blueberry pancakes?''

Later that afternoon, Skye loaded her mother's suitcase into the trunk of her car and got ready to drive her back to the hospital. After lunch, Dawn had gone to Skye's sister Alice's house to play with her three children, so there would be just the two of them in the car.

Skye walked into the house and found her mother hanging up the phone.

"There's been a change in plans," Marge Williamson said.

Skye felt as though she'd swallowed a rock. "Is Daddy all right?"

"He's the same, but they've had another patient come into the emergency room with a hand injury and Doc wants him to see a microsurgeon as soon as possible, so they're sending him to San Antonio in the helicopter with your father. But Doc also managed to find me another way to the city. Wasn't that sweet of him?''

"He knows you're the best medicine Daddy could have.''

Marge gave her daughter a hug, then picked up her tote bag-size purse and headed for the door. "We'd better get going.''

"Where?"

"I need you to drive me out to the Diamond S," Marge told her. "Clint Slade has offered the use of his plane and pilot."

Skye managed to keep her cool and act normally because she fully expected Clint would be busy elsewhere on the ranch and not anywhere near the airstrip.

Once they were on the road, her mother reached into her purse and took out her knitting. Marge rarely sat in one spot for long, but when she did, there was always mending or knitting in her hands. Six years hadn't changed Marge much, although more white was in her hair. She looked tired, but Skye assumed it was from the stress of having her husband in the hospital.

The rhythmic click of knitting needles was a soothing sound to Skye, bringing back memories.

"Dawn is a well-behaved little girl," Marge said after a while.

Skye caught her bottom lip between her teeth and kept her eyes on the road. "Thanks."

She felt a twinge of regret that today was the first time her mother and daughter had been together. Her own grandparents had been so special to her during her childhood, she was sad Dawn hadn't had the same benefit.

Along with the twinge of regret, Skye felt a hefty dose of guilt. She quickly forced herself to shove the guilt away. Although her father's mandate had sent her away, her mother hadn't stood up to him on her behalf.

Blaming and pointing fingers was useless at this point. It wouldn't accomplish anything, but neither would shouldering *all* the guilt herself, even though it felt instinctive to do just that.

Her mother set down her knitting and turned toward Skye. "I wish I could have watched her grow up." Her voice was thick with emotion.

Skye swallowed past the lump in her own throat. "Mama, don't. Unless you want me driving down the highway all weepy-eyed."

"No, I don't want that, but I want you to know I wish things had been different."

Don't we all?

"Wishing isn't going to change anything about the past," Skye said. "At the moment, we need to focus on Daddy getting well and keeping the businesses running smoothly." And getting herself and Dawn back home without Clint accidentally discovering he had a daughter.

"You're right, dear. And thank you for coming."

"You're welcome."

When they reached the airstrip, the first person Skye spotted was Clint.

No man should look so good in denim!

To distract herself, Skye gave all her attention to unlocking and opening the trunk of her car. Reminding herself she was here to drop off her mother, not check out the too-handsome, too-sexy, unapproachable Mr. Slade.

Except Mr. Slade had been pretty darned approachable last night when they'd been pressed together kissing in the parking lot. Too darned approachable!

"Let me get that." Clint stepped up beside her, took the suitcase and carried it to the plane.

Skye and Marge said their goodbyes, then Marge and the pilot entered the plane, leaving Skye and Clint alone. They stood side by side and watched quietly until the plane took to the sky and headed southeast.

Skye turned in Clint's direction, keeping her eyes on the snap buttons of his shirt, until she found herself thinking about the hard wall of male muscle behind it. Then she moved her gaze to meet his. "We appreciate your pilot flying Mom to be with Dad."

"Glad to be of service." He tucked his hands into the back pockets of his well-worn blue jeans, drawing Skye's focus and thoughts off on another tangent she didn't want them taking. "Are you heading back to town?"

No, I'm going to stand here and look at you all day.

She cleared her throat. "Y-yes."

"I have a few boxes at the house that need to be dropped off at the community center, if you're not in a hurry."

"I have time. It's the least I can do after what you've done for Mom."

She hoped the boxes weren't a ploy to pick up where they'd left off in the parking lot last night. Didn't she?

Skye followed the cloud of dust raised by Clint's truck to the ranch house. The house was a showplace of

sand-colored stucco and red tile roof. Skye had seen it
before when she'd attended the rodeos held at the Diamond S. She wondered if Clint lived there with his parents or had his own place somewhere else.

"Come on in," Clint said.

"I can wait out here while you get the boxes. I
wouldn't want to intrude on your parents."

"My parents don't live here anymore. Dad retired a
few years ago. They bought a motor home and took off.
They've been traveling all over the country."

She wondered if he'd lived alone since his divorce.
She shied away from prying. Yet she wanted to know.
And she wanted to see inside the house.

Dawn's father's house.

Something tugged deep within her as she realized
again how little she knew about this man. He was the
father of her child, but he was a virtual stranger.

What sort of a man was he? What was his favorite
color? What kind of books did he like? In the evenings, did he read, watch sitcoms, PBS, rent videos? Or
did he spend his evenings with women?

Before she could even think about Chuck's sugges-
tion that she tell Clint about Dawn, she needed to know
more about him. But how could she get to know him
without ending up in his arms? She already knew all she
needed about the way he kissed and her susceptibility to
him physically.

Clint gestured toward the front door. "Shall we?"

Inside, the house was a showplace, too. The South-
west decor looked perfect against the rugged splendor

of the Texas countryside seen through large picture windows across the back wall.

"It's beautiful," Skye said.

"It's my mother's doing. I haven't changed much since they moved out. Would you like the fifty-cent tour?"

She would love the chance to see the rest of the house, but knew she'd be crazy to put herself in the position of being alone with Clint anywhere near his, or any other, bedroom. If he took it in mind to kiss her, she was in deep trouble. She wondered again if that might be the whole reason he'd asked her here.

"I need to be getting back to town."

"Tell you what. I'll leave the offer open."

"Thanks."

"I'll just get those boxes." He headed down a hall leading off to the left through a curved archway.

Skye stepped out of the entry hall and down into the living room. It was so different from the homey atmosphere of the Williamson house and even more different from the small living room that did double duty as her bedroom in the apartment she shared with Dawn.

Dawn . . . little Dawn was related to all this. Skye pictured her curled in the corner of the oversize couch, singing to her stuffed animals. Or kneeling beside the coffee table drawing pictures and coloring them with her crayons.

"Skye?"

Clint's voice broke into her thoughts. He was standing in the entry hall, holding two boxes, one on top of the other.

"Let me get the door for you," she said.

He smiled, the warm sexy smile that sent her pulse racing. "I was hoping you'd offer."

Once the boxes were tucked into her car, Skye turned to Clint. For a fleeting moment, she wished herself alone, unencumbered, free to pursue the desire she could see in his eyes. The next moment, a boulder of guilt crashed down on her and she was overwhelmed by the urge to rush to town and hug her daughter close to her heart.

"Darlin', are you all right?"

She smiled and tried to look normal. "This has been such a hectic week. So much has happened since I heard about Dad."

"Things seem to be working out. He's off for tests and you said you've had plenty of people applying for jobs."

"Yes, it is working out, and I'm grateful . . . on my way here, I was so frightened I might be on my way to a funeral—" Her voice broke as she allowed herself to say the words that until that moment had only echoed in her thoughts.

Clint gathered her into his arms. The unexpected offer of comfort surprised Skye. Surprised her, then touched her deeply. Deeply enough she wasn't able to hold back the tears.

While Clint held her close, rubbing her back and murmuring words of comfort, she cried. Cried with relief that her fears for her father's life had been premature. Cried with sadness for the lost years when they'd been estranged, and with joy that they might still have a chance to set things right between them.

There were also tears for her daughter, who was growing up without a father in her life. One or two tears of self-pity slipped out, too, before she stopped them.

After a while, the flow of tears slowed, but she stayed in Clint's arms, soaking up comfort and strength. The sexy, confident cowboy had disappeared, leaving in his place a sympathetic, compassionate man. Skye closed her eyes. A calming peacefulness settled over her. When was the last time she'd felt so serene?

With a sigh, she straightened and looked at him. "I'm sorry for falling apart on you."

He tucked her hair behind her ears and brushed at the remnants of moisture on her cheeks. "Nothing to be sorry about. The way I see it, you've earned the right to a few tears."

"Maybe. But you shouldn't have to put up with them."

He smiled. It was a warm smile, not his usual cocky grin. "Any time you need a shoulder to cry on, you know where to find me."

"Thanks." She started to move out of his arms, then on impulse, she went on tiptoe to kiss his cheek. His skin was warm against her lips.

Clint took the friendly gesture a step further by returning the kiss—not on her cheek, but on her lips. It was whisper-soft at first, only increasing in pressure when she didn't pull away. As the kiss grew, all the sparks she'd felt last night were back in force.

She parted her lips. He deepened the kiss gradually. The saltiness of drying tears mingled with the taste of desire. Her knees felt wobbly. The heat and passion between them was there as always. But coming as it did on top of the calm from his comforting her, a whole new dimension was added. They were connecting more than as male to female, and for more reason than the sexual chemistry between them. This afternoon, they had crossed a line between being just acquaintances and the beginnings of friendship. The change lent an increased intimacy to the kiss.

Clint straightened, breaking the contact. Skye looked into his eyes, dazed.

"Like I said, if you need a shoulder to cry on, you know where to find me."

She moved back. He loosened his hold until his hands rested on either side of her waist.

She smiled, nodding her thanks this time. He helped her into the car and she set off, a deep sense of peace and well-being wrapped around her like a warm blanket on a cold night.

But the comfort was short-lived as words from yesterday morning's conversation with her brother came back to haunt her.

He has a right to know. He's her father for crying out loud.

She stuck to her belief that a lot of men would rather not be told about an unwanted pregnancy, but she was no longer sure Clint Slade was one of them.

Four

Clint watched Skye drive away until all he could see was a dust cloud on the distant horizon. He glanced at his shirt. The wet patch was already drying around the edges—dampness left by Skye's tears.

It had felt strange, but good, holding her. Between the long hours he devoted to the ranch and his hundred-mile rule, holding a woman in his arms wasn't something he did often.

He'd been holding Skye to console her, to let her know he cared. That he honestly cared was strange, too. She was probably setting him up, but that hadn't stopped him from feeling her pain. His ex-wife had played him for a fool, he sure hoped Skye wasn't getting ready to do the same.

Regardless of what she might have planned, her pain this afternoon had been real and he didn't regret offering her what little comfort he could.

His thoughts wandered to the kiss. It had been as explosive and staggering as the one last night. Keeping his hormones on a tight rein had been a challenge. But only a cold-blooded snake would have taken advantage of her vulnerable state by pushing for anything more than a few kisses.

His hormones had cooperated, but he couldn't stop his mind from picturing the two of them tucked away between his sheets—goin' at it hot and heavy or curled around each other in sated exhaustion. Both images held a certain appeal.

He wondered how long Skye would be staying in Harmony Ridge.

Skye stopped by the community center to drop off Clint's boxes. A group of local women were busy sorting items for an upcoming rummage sale.

Jean Bartlett, the reverend's wife, showed Skye where to put the boxes. "Clint Slade is such a dear. He always comes through for us."

Mrs. Holter, one of the other women helping spoke up, "He's agreed to be chairman of the junior rodeo again this year."

"Yes, I'd heard that," Jean said. "I can't believe someone hasn't snatched that man up yet."

A few other women exchanged some whispered comments, which Skye didn't catch in full. She caught enough to know that they were also singing Clint's praises. But for things they didn't want the reverend's wife to overhear.

A dull ache started behind her temples. The depiction of Clint as a sought-after pillar of the community made it seem even more likely that he was the type of man who would want to know about any child he might have fathered.

If she was going to tell him about Dawn, it would be easier to do before someone *did* snatch him up. She needed to get away and do some thinking.

Skye started to say her goodbyes, but it took her longer to leave than she'd hoped. Everyone wanted to hear the latest news of her father and how things were going for the Williamsons. The only subject she strayed from was the question of why she'd left town, letting them think her new job had lured her away.

It was nice getting updates on old friends, too. After high school, she'd drifted away from most of them as she took on more hours at the coffee shop and her friends went off to college or got married. She hadn't thought about them in a long time, but it was good to hear familiar names and news of where life had taken them the past six years.

After she was through at the community center, she stopped by Alice's to pick up Dawn, but ended up consenting to let her spend the night with her cousins.

Back at her parents' home, as she went through the rest of the afternoon and early evening, her mind kept drifting to thoughts of being in Clint's arms. What would it feel like to know that such a haven would be there each and every time she needed it? Life would be easier if she had the security of someone to lean on now and then.

She'd been asked out over the years by dude ranch guests and her co-workers, but had never seriously considered accepting any of the invitations. Maybe it was time she did.

Sure, Skye, like any ol' guy could compare to Clint!

With Dawn not home, Skye went to the coffee shop earlier than usual. It was only the second day of training the new employees, but the task was pretty much finished. Two of the people had worked at the Rocking W before retiring and they'd helped with the teaching. The regular customers threw in their two cents' worth, as well.

While putting out new place settings in a recently vacated booth, Skye noticed a ruckus in the parking lot by the bar. She needed a closer look at the situation before deciding whether or not to call the sheriff. Quickly, she slipped out the back door. From this angle, she could see her oldest brother, Beau, toward the rear of the crowd. He was smiling, so she figured everything must be under control.

Since she was due for a break, she wandered over to see what all the fuss was about. When the crowd shifted, she caught a glimpse of Chuck and several local cowboys showing off their roping skills.

Skye stood next to Beau and cheered Chuck on for a while, then turned to go back to work.

"Hey, Chuck. Moving target," Beau yelled.

When they'd been kids, a call of "moving target" meant one of the sisters was about to become a target for whatever competition the brothers were involved in. But they weren't kids anymore.

He wouldn't dare!

A quick glance over her shoulder proved that yes, he would. Skye started to run, but it was too little and too late. A roar of good-natured cheering and teasing rose from the crowd while Chuck slowly reeled her in. She knew better than to scream or fight him, it would only prolong things.

"Auction her off." The comment, from somewhere in the crowd, set off another round of laughter.

Skye almost laughed, herself, until her gaze locked with Clint's. He was leaning against a wooden fence, one ankle crossed over the other, arms folded over his broad chest. Casually, his gaze roamed down her body, as though she *were* for sale and he was considering how much to offer. No neighborly concern in this look—it was hot and loaded with sexual overtones. Her breath caught in her throat and a shiver worked its way along her spine.

It was a forceful reminder that she was missing more than the safe haven of comforting arms by living without a man in her life.

Luckily, the spell was broken when she reached Chuck and Clint was blocked from view.

"I need to get back to the coffee shop, Chuck."

Her brother picked her up, slung her over his shoulder and started across the parking lot. "We wouldn't want you to be late for work, would we?"

Skye caught one last glimpse of Clint. Dang the man, he was smiling. And right before the crowd blocked him from view, he tipped his hat to her.

Clint wished he was the one with Skye slung over his shoulder. And he sure wouldn't be carrying her back to work. Especially since the reason he'd come to town was to lure her away for a while.

When he'd first climbed into his pickup, he'd told himself Skye needed a break. Along the way, he'd admitted he was anxious to check that she'd fully recovered from her emotional outpouring this afternoon. By the time he'd arrived at the Rocking W, he acknowledged his reasons for coming were both of those, and also because he simply wanted to see her.

Maybe the last reason was most important of all....

He watched a few more rounds of the impromptu roping contest then made his way into the coffee shop. The place was busy with the dinner crowd. He nodded in response to greetings and answered, "All right" to questions of "How're things goin'?"

He made his way across the room and took a seat in an empty booth next to one where Skye was filling coffee cups for two elderly couples.

"Coffee?" She didn't quite meet his gaze when she stepped over to wait on him.

"Sure."

Her hand shook slightly as she poured.

She didn't seem to be in the same frame of mind she'd been in before her overflowing emotions this afternoon. Instead, she was back to the aloofness he'd sensed the night he'd been in for pie. He was usually good at reading women, too. Not being able to figure out Skye was frustrating. Frustrating, but he had to admit that lent an element of challenge to the chase.

"What's the special tonight?"

Wouldn't it be a kicker if she said she was?

"Chicken-fried steak."

He ordered. Skye went back to work. He followed her with his gaze. After she delivered his meal, he ate slowly and continued watching her. By the time he was finished, the restaurant had cleared out somewhat.

"Dessert?" she asked as she came up to his booth.

"No, thanks." The only sweet thing he was craving at the moment was one of Skye's kisses.

She set his bill on the edge of the table.

"What time do you get off tonight?"

"I don't have a set quitting time."

"Any chance you could sneak off now?"

"Now?"

"Yeah, I'd like to take you dancing."

Dancing was a spur-of-the-moment notion, but he had to admit it was a helluva good idea. She would get some unwinding time and he would get the pleasure of holding her in his arms.

Clint rested his open hand on her lower back as they walked into the Rocking W Bar. More than one person spotted the pair and nudged the person next to them. In no time, it seemed as though more people were watching them than the band.

Chuck, who was behind the bar with Beau, gave her an especially pointed look. She could imagine what wheels his mind was spinning. What if he said something about a supposed earlier relationship between her and Clint? If she was lucky, Clint would write it off as a mistake on Chuck's part. If she wasn't lucky, Clint would have a whole bunch of questions that wouldn't be easy to answer.

Her sister, Heather, who was waiting tables, also watched with interest. Only Beau seemed to be minding his own business.

Why did you agree to this craziness, Skye? she admonished herself.

Because she hadn't been able to say no. Against her better judgment, she was drawn to Clint. Perhaps it was leftover fragments of her long-ago crush. Then again, it might be the need to know her daughter's father. Or maybe the pure and simple fact that when he smiled his too-sexy smile and asked nicely with that deep, smooth drawl, *yes* was the only word in her vocabulary.

She couldn't trust herself around him. Too much depended on his behavior and she didn't have any idea what to expect from him this evening.

This afternoon when they'd been alone together, Clint had held her in comfort and had given her a tender kiss. But as he'd proved on other occasions, he could turn up the heat and kiss her senseless.

He'd been a perfect gentleman in the coffee shop, but the look he'd given her as Chuck had carried her off hadn't been the least bit gentlemanly. Which side of the man was going to be there tonight?

Which one did she want?

The answer to that question was important, but downright scary.

"Shall we dance, or would you like to get a table?" Clint asked.

If they sat down, she would be anticipating the moment when they would stand toe-to-toe and she would put her hand in his. The best thing would be to get it over with so she didn't have to spend time worrying.

"Let's dance."

He led her to the dance floor. The first awkward moment passed. Skye concentrated on the music and following Clint's lead in the two-step. He didn't go in for a lot of fancy moves, but he knew the basic steps and had a good sense of rhythm.

The band's set was a mix of upbeat tunes with an occasional slow song thrown in. Clint took the slower tempos as an excuse to pull her closer.

They weren't the only couple in a tight clinch, so instead of trying to move away, she settled in and enjoyed it. She might as well, she decided, since she had the security of a roomful of people to guarantee things couldn't get carried away.

She rested her cheek against his chest. He rested his cheek against her hair. The brim of his hat created an intimate shield blocking out the rest of the room. Hip to hip, Skye felt clear evidence that Clint's full attention wasn't on the music or the dance steps.

And yours is? she asked herself silently.

It didn't help matters that this song had been the one playing on the truck radio the night she and Clint had made love six years ago. Her eyes started the tingling that signaled tears. Refusing to give in again, she closed them and blocked out the memories by focusing on the sheer pleasure of dancing with Clint.

Too soon the last notes of the song faded. The band announced it would be taking a break.

"Would you like something to drink?" Clint asked.

Skye wanted to talk to him. She owed it to Dawn to get to know him better. Besides, the better she knew him, the easier it should be to decide whether or not to tell him about Dawn.

The chances of their being able to have a private conversation in the crowded bar were doubtful. While she liked the security of having other people around, she didn't like the idea of them listening in. They would have the same problem if they went to the coffee shop. Her aunt and uncle were at the house, but there was the wooden swing on the front porch.

"It's been a long day. Would you settle for iced tea at the house?" she replied. He raised one dark eyebrow and she added, "On the front porch."

"Fine by me."

He took her hand and started for the door. Their exit wasn't as smooth as their entrance. The shock of their being there together had apparently worn off, and they were stopped along the way by a number of folks. Some welcomed Skye home, others had this or that to ask Clint.

They finally made it to the door and stepped out into the night. Even though it was almost summer and the days were hot, a chill was in the high-desert night air. A crescent moon and stars gleamed against the sky's inky blackness.

They walked across the parking lot to the Williamson's house. Skye left Clint on the porch while she went into the kitchen to get the drinks. When she returned, he was sitting on one side of the swing. His long legs were stretched in front of him and he used them to gently rock the swing back and forth.

He stopped the motion long enough for Skye to join him. She handed him his glass.

"Thanks." He took a long swallow.

Skye sipped hers then leaned over to set the glass on the porch railing.

The sound of the band starting to play again drifted across the parking lot.

"The band was pretty good tonight," Skye said.

"As good as any you'd hear in the city."

"I wouldn't know."

"You mean, you didn't leave Harmony Ridge because things are bigger and better in the city?"

"No. In fact, the dude ranch where I work is even farther from civilization than Harmony Ridge."

She'd always liked the small town where she'd been born, and probably wouldn't have left if her father hadn't believed so fervently that her being an unwed mother would be a disgrace to their family.

"I figured it was probably closer. Most people who leave here go searching for someplace more exciting."

"Is that what Teresa did?"

He moved his glass to his lips. Skye thought he wasn't going to answer, but after taking a drink he said, "She moved to Houston."

"I'm sorry."

"Don't be. I'm not."

He sounded more resigned than hurt. Maybe the passage of time had healed his wounds. Lucky him. She wished she could say the same.

"You two seemed so...so much in love."

"I suppose we did." He took another drink, then set his glass beside hers, the action causing his shoulder to brush against her.

"You did. I...we all figured it was a match made in heaven." The thought had made her unhappy, but she hadn't doubted it for a second.

"Looks can be deceiving."

"If you two weren't in love, why did you ask her to marry you?"

He looked at her, long and hard. "I can't speak for Teresa, but I was positively convinced that I was in love when I got married."

Hearing him say the words, she hurt now almost as much as she had when she'd first learned of his engagement. But she wasn't the only one hurting. She could hear pain in Clint's voice and see it in his eyes. She reached out her hand and rested it on his arm. He placed his larger one over hers.

"When did you realize you weren't?"

"It didn't take long."

"How?"

He looked into the darkness, then back at her. "I'd rather not talk about it."

She wanted to ask more questions, to hear all the details. In a way, she felt that he owed her an explanation. She'd given up her family, friends and her hometown so he could live happily ever after with the woman of his dreams.

As the reality of his divorce became clearer to her, she realized her sacrifices had all been for nothing.

She felt cheated. "You're right. It isn't any of my business."

Clint tightened his hand around hers. "Don't take it wrong, darlin'. I don't mind your asking. I just don't want to talk about it." He shifted his grip until their hands rested palm-to-palm. "For what it's worth, I've told you more about it than I've ever told anyone else."

"Why?"

"I wish I knew." He sifted a strand of her hair through his fingers. "What about you? Have you ever been married?"

"No."

"Ever gotten close?"

She shrugged. Before leaving town, she would have married Clint if he'd asked her instead of Teresa. But she suspected that wouldn't count. "No."

They rocked without talking for a while. The squeak of the swing's chains sometimes matched the rhythm of the distant music, and sometimes sounded horribly offbeat.

"If you didn't leave Harmony Ridge in search of big-city excitement, why did you leave?" he asked after a moment.

The truth was perched on the tip of her tongue. With the beauty of the night and the warm security of having her hand in Clint's, the truth wanted to tumble out.

Luckily, only a small piece of it escaped. "It seemed like the best thing to do at the time."

"Sounds as though you have regrets."

"I guess I do."

Not the ones he supposed, but yes, she had plenty of regrets.

"Have you given any thought to moving back?"

"No."

His question and her answer made her realize how completely she'd shut herself off from Harmony Ridge the night she'd left, mentally burning the bridge between her old home and the new one she'd been heading for. She'd made a complete break.

"How much longer are you staying?"

"A few more days."

"Not much time left then," he said.

There wasn't much time for her to decide whether to tell Clint about Dawn this trip. But that couldn't be what he was talking about.

"Much time left for what?"

"For this."

He reached an arm around her shoulder and pulled her closer to him. With his other hand, he tilted her chin up until he found the perfect angle, then he lowered his head until his mouth lay over hers.

No, there wasn't much time left for this, either. Maybe it was for the best, considering the way his slightest touch set off a deep yearning inside her. It wasn't the yearning she minded so much—it felt good— but it bothered her to know that dropping her guard and finding fulfillment for her awakened needs was impossible.

A sigh escaped her as she submitted to the kiss despite the frustration she knew would follow when the contact ended.

Clint adjusted his legs, then scooped her up and settled her across his lap. Skye slipped her arms around his neck, running her fingers over hard male muscle and the soft wavy ends of his hair.

Their gazes met and held as they adjusted to their new positions, then he kissed her again. A long, slow kiss— he tasted and teased with his mouth and tongue.

Skye sighed again and Clint deepened the kiss, increasing the pressure, driving deeper, entwining his tongue with hers. Supporting her with one arm, he brought the other between them and made short work of the buttons on her blouse. He folded open the sides, then placed a tantalizing trail of kisses from her mouth to the edge of her bra.

Instinctively, she arched toward him. He traced the lacy boundary with more kisses and an occasional sweep of his tongue. Her bra suddenly felt uncomfortably tight as her breasts swelled and her lungs fought for each ragged breath.

With a flick of his fingers, Clint opened the front clasp, releasing the pressure and uncovering her to his gaze. He stroked his fingers over her in tantalizing patterns as he looked his fill.

He gave a slow whistle.

His obvious appreciation sent a thrill through Skye. With the increase in her feminine confidence, she set out on her own sensual exploration.

Unsnapping the pearl-covered fasteners on Clint's western shirt, she exposed his tanned, hair-covered chest. As she made the opening wider, her fingers brushed through the dark curls. Her fingertips made only brief contact with the skin beneath, but it was enough for her to feel the intense heat radiating from him. He felt so hot, almost feverish.

The heat sparked the memory of their long-ago lovemaking, the feel of his warmth lowering toward and settling along the length of her until she'd felt completely surrounded.

Clint stroked his fingertips down the sides of her breasts. "Let's go inside."

"My aunt and uncle are here, in the living room," Skye said.

Clint groaned. Leaning forward, he opened his mouth over one tight peak. For a moment, Skye considered trying to sneak him up to her room by climbing the oak tree next to the window.

Then Clint shifted his attention to her other breast and for a moment she couldn't think at all.

"We'll have to drive to my place. Except . . . I'm not sure I'll be able to make it out of the parking lot, darlin', and I'd hate for our first time to be in the front seat of my pickup."

Five

The front seat of his pickup.

Clint's remark killed the mood as much as the arrival of a stampede would have. Skye jumped out of his lap. Not bothering with her bra, she had her blouse buttoned in record time.

"Clint, I can't . . . we can't . . . I'm so sorry."

She muttered a hasty good-night then raced into the house before he could stop her.

Her own body had become a stranger to her—a traitorous stranger. She wanted to make love with Clint. Lord, how she wanted to. And he wanted to make love, too.

Make love to her . . . Skye.

He wasn't drunk, he knew who she was this time and he wanted her!

It was years too late and impossible for her to follow up on, but it was still a sweet victory.

She made her way upstairs, to the bathroom and into the shower. That long-ago night when she and Clint had made love, the house had been empty when she'd made the same trek. Back then, as the water had flowed over her, she'd been aware of the achy soreness between her legs and the ultrasensitive state of her nipples.

Tonight, the feelings were the same from the waist up, but the aching from the waist down was from unfulfilled desire. A sad, empty feeling. In its own way as painful as the aftermath of their first lovemaking.

After drying off, she wrapped a towel around herself and went to her room. It felt empty without Dawn. But it was just as well the little girl wasn't there. She would be a reminder of her daddy... the too-sexy cowboy.

Skye slipped a nightgown over her head and climbed into bed. Her mind was still busy with images of Clint—the night they'd made love and tonight's interlude on the swing. The thoughts were physically unsettling, so she forced her mind to think back farther to other nights she'd ended the day in this bed.

Even after "lights out," she, Heather and Alice would talk. They got along well and didn't mind sharing their room until the 4-H barbecue at the J Bar T. Teresa Donnelly had made sure everyone saw the blue ribbon she'd won at a horse show in San Antonio the weekend before. The ribbon had been impressive, but

Skye hadn't found it nearly as interesting as Teresa's bedroom.

It was twice the size of theirs, frilly and feminine, the ideal little girl's room. Skye had immediately fallen in love with the ruffle-covered, canopied bed. There was also a matching dresser, vanity table, corner desk and bookshelf, which held more riding trophies and ribbons than books.

At home, later that night, Alice had been the first to say how nice it would be if they each had their own room. Skye and Heather had agreed. From that night on, before drifting to sleep, Skye would gaze at the bottom of the mattress above and pretend it was a ruffled canopy.

The perfect bedroom wasn't the only thing Teresa had had that the Williamson sisters didn't. She had horses, a swimming pool and she'd grown up to become Mrs. Clint Slade.

But only for five months.

They must have been getting divorced about the time Dawn was cutting her first tooth. For the first time, Skye let herself wonder what might have happened if she hadn't left town that night six years ago.

What if she'd told Clint about the baby before his marriage? Or what if she'd gone to him right after his divorce? Would there have been a chance for the two of them? Well, the three of them, if she counted Dawn.

Her plan to head home within the next few days weighed heavily on her. If she was going to tell Clint about Dawn, it was going to have to be soon.

She would be back to visit when her father was released from the hospital, but the thought of postponing her decision until then didn't appeal to her. For her own peace of mind, it would be best to decide as soon as possible, which was easier said than done.

She tried to imagine what Clint's reaction would be. What if he didn't want to have anything to do with Dawn? It was possible. She had no idea whether he liked children at all, and some men were into that macho gotta-have-a-son-first routine.

What if Clint thought she was telling him just to get child support? If he offered, she would tell him to keep his money. They were doing all right without it. But a more sensible, less prideful voice reminded her the school year was coming and Dawn was going to need new clothes.

If he offered money, she might accept it.

What if he offers more?

More ... like marriage and a home for the three of them and the possibility of brothers and sisters for Dawn.

Get real, Skye. What were the chances of that happening? Slim to none.

And Slim just left town, as they would have said in high school.

Despite the unlikeliness of it happening, Skye let herself envision what it would be like to be married to Clint. Plenty of cozy family moments.

And what else, honey? Be real honest, now.

Fine, she would admit it—the thought of ending each day by getting into bed with Clint had a certain appeal. Making love with him, drifting off to sleep in his arms, waking him with kisses.

She realized then that in her heart, she'd already decided to tell Clint about their daughter.

The next morning, Skye drove over to Alice's to pick up Dawn. She was only somewhat surprised that her sister knew she'd been dancing at the Rocking W Bar last night with Clint.

"So, is this the start of something?" Alice asked.

"It wasn't a date or anything. He had dinner at the coffee shop and then asked if I wanted to go dancing."

"There has to be more to it."

More? Like almost making love on the front porch? What would Alice have to say to that? What would Chuck have said if he'd come home from work early? The thought hadn't occurred to her until now.

"No, no more than that," Skye answered.

"Clint Slade rarely comes into the bar these days. And when he does show up, he's alone and he leaves alone."

From the looks the women were giving him last night, Skye figured if Clint was alone then it must be by choice. "He didn't jump back into the girl-of-the-month club he had going before his engagement to Teresa?"

Alice shook her head. "Strange, huh? There were rumors about him and some woman from Dallas, but nothing seemed to come of it."

"Maybe he doesn't have time now that he's running the ranch."

"He made time last night."

Skye shrugged. "Don't read too much into it." She wasn't sure whether her warning was meant for Alice or herself.

Later that afternoon, Skye called Clint.

"What can I do for you?" He didn't sound too surprised to hear from her.

"I was wondering if you might have a free moment this evening."

"Change your mind about going to the movies?"

It took her a moment to remember he'd suggested they catch a movie, the first evening they'd talked in the coffee shop. Her thoughts were more focused on the interlude they'd shared on the front porch last night. "No, I have something I want to discuss with you."

"Uh-huh."

"Could we meet somewhere?" She wished for neutral ground, but everywhere she'd considered there was the possibility they would be seen or overheard. The least she could do for Clint was to give him the chance to react openly and honestly when she dropped her bombshell.

"Name the place and time."

"I was hoping for someplace where we could talk without being interrupted."

"My place?"

It wasn't exactly neutral, but there would be privacy from prying eyes.

"All right. How's six-thirty?" Once they talked, it would still be early enough for him to come back to her parents' house, meet Dawn and spend time with her. That is, if he wanted to.

"Would you like me to pick you up? I'll take a cold shower before leaving the house so we'll be able to get here before I ravish you." Skye could hear the laughter in his voice.

After the way she'd responded to him last night and now asked to meet somewhere private, then agreeing to go to his house, it was logical for him to assume that she planned to spend the evening making love with him.

"This isn't a date, Clint. I'm just coming to talk." How nice it would be if this *were* as simple as a date. "I'll drive myself to the ranch."

"All right." Did he sound skeptical, or was it her overactive imagination thinking he did? "Will you stay for dinner?"

She couldn't even bear the thought of food. "No, thanks."

"I'll see you this evening."

She replaced the receiver, praying she'd made the right decision.

Clint hung up the phone. Leather creaked as he leaned back in his desk chair.

What in tarnation was up with Skye?

He'd planned on calling her later, but she'd beat him to it. That was a good sign, actually. After last night, he thought he was going to have his work cut out for him trying to convince her to see him again. He wasn't sure what had gone wrong, but he intended to find out.

The sexual sparks had been flying, but they'd shut down faster than he would have believed possible. He'd replayed the scene over and over. The only solution that seemed to make any sense was that Skye must be a virgin.

She didn't kiss like a virgin...not at all. And the way she'd let him open her blouse and opened his shirt in return hadn't shown an inch of shyness.

It was obvious she'd wanted him. If they'd been somewhere more private, he doubted if they would have stopped. Clothes would have kept coming off and he would have made love to her and her seductive body that had been haunting him since he'd stopped for coffee... Had it only been four nights ago?

Tonight there would be no need to stop or change locations for any reason. He made a mental note to be sure to put a condom in his pocket before six-thirty.

On second thought...make that two.

Dawn was clearly disappointed when Skye told her she was going out alone for a while. She knew the possibility of meeting her father would put a smile on the little girl's face, but what if Clint didn't want to meet her? It was wiser not to say anything to her just yet.

She told Chuck, though. He seemed pleased with her decision and volunteered to baby-sit.

Nervous wreck was a total understatement of her condition by the time she brought her car to a stop in front of Clint's house. In keeping with the "no date" image, she'd dressed casually in blue jeans, boots and a sleeveless blue blouse that buttoned up the front.

Clint opened the front door as she started up the walkway. He must have been listening or watching for her. He tipped his hat as she reached him.

They settled in the living room. Skye turned down his offer of soda or a drink.

"So, what can I do for you?"

Skye looked at Clint, gazing deep into his eyes, and froze. Words flew through her brain in flashes, but none made their way out her mouth. Dawn's words added to the confusion—"My daddy, the cowboy"—playing over and over in her mind.

Yes, this man watching her so intently with a puzzled look was Dawn's daddy, the cowboy. . . .

"I don't know where to begin," she said.

"The beginning is usually best," Clint said.

But was it in this case? The beginning was the desperate unrequited crush she'd had on Clint growing up. It wouldn't accomplish anything other than her embarrassment to admit it to him.

"Well . . ." Skye rubbed her palms across her blue jeans, then realized her hands were trembling.

Clint must have noticed, too, because he stood, closed the distance between them and took her hands in his. Gently, he pulled her up, then led her to the couch, settling them both into the large cushions. He placed her still-trembling hands flat against his chest and used his own to soothe her from elbows to fingertips.

"Calm down, darlin'."

She took a deep breath. The scent of his after-shave washed over her.

"That's it, just relax." Clint shifted his hands around to continue his stroking motions along her back. Each stroke moved her closer to him. "This is going to be your first time, isn't it?"

She pulled back. "I told you on the phone that's not why I wanted to see you."

Like he's supposed to believe that when the first thing you do is melt into his arms.

"Darlin', it's nothing to be shy or ashamed about. I know it's rare for a woman to be a virgin at your age, and I understand your being nervous, but—"

Skye stood and moved across the room to stand by the window. "I'm not a virgin, Clint."

"Well...okay...that's all right, too. I just thought that might be why you panicked last night."

Skye turned to look out the picture window, her eyes focused on the mountains lining the horizon. "I have a daughter."

Reflected in the glass, she saw Clint stand and walk toward her. When he reached her, he turned her to face him, tipping her chin up with his fingers. "And you think that makes a difference to me? I'm not one of those guys who refuses to date women with children."

"That's only part of the problem, Clint."

"Is her father still in the picture?"

Skye took a deep breath and held it briefly. She sent up a silent prayer to the powers that be.

Please, let him be happy about this.

"Clint—" Her voice broke. She cleared her throat and finished the sentence. "You're Dawn's father."

He took a step back, looking at her as though she'd lost her mind. "Darlin', you must have missed school the day they taught about the birds and the bees. It takes more than kisses, no matter how hot, and a lot longer than a few days for two people to make a baby."

"I know how babies get here. Dawn's not a baby. She's five years old."

He shook his head. "Just what are you trying to pull?"

"I'm not trying to pull anything. I'm just trying to tell you that you have a daughter."

Clint crossed his arms over his chest and scowled at her. "Look, if you want to borrow money, just say so. Don't go making up cockamamy stories about me being the father of your child when we both know you and I never slept together! Hell, I didn't even know who you were when I saw you the other night at the coffee shop, but you're telling me we've *done it*."

"This isn't about money."

"Oh, please."

"I thought you should know." Despite all her careful consideration of the matter, she was beginning to think she'd made a mistake.

"You thought I should know?" He gave a harsh laugh. "Listen, I'm sorry about your dad, I'm sorry you got yourself knocked up and have to raise a child on your own. But there's no way I'm going to let you trick me into thinking the kid is mine."

"Why would I make up something like this?"

"For the money, obviously."

"I told you, this isn't about money."

"Sorry, but I have a real tough time believing that."

No amount of money was worth her having to stand here and have him look at her with the same scorn he'd give something nasty stuck to the bottom of his boot. "With all the fancy DNA technology that can establish paternity, I'd have to be pretty stupid to make up something like this."

"You said it, honey, I didn't."

She could feel the blood drain from her face. He didn't believe her. He flat out didn't believe her. She could try to spark his memory of that night, but in his current mood he would probably accuse her of making it up.

Meeting Dawn might convince him, but what would it do to the little girl if he showed up once and then never came again?

"I need to be getting back," she said abruptly. "Dawn and I will be heading for home in a few days. If you decide you'd like to meet her, give me a call."

She doubted she'd hear from him.

Clint was lit.

"Of all the low-down, miserable, pathetic tricks anyone has ever tried to pull on me," he railed, pacing the living room.

Oh, and she had her routine down, too. Setting the stage with her phone call, knowing he wouldn't believe she just wanted to talk. Acting insecure, making him feel all softhearted at her insecurity, then crawling into his arms and getting his body primed hard enough to drive nails.

Once she had him where she wanted, she'd tried to snap the trap shut. And she'd been going for much more than a simple loan. Bringing a kid into the scam meant she was looking for something on a monthly basis... eighteen-plus years of it.

He stormed out to the barn, saddled Zeus, packed the saddlebags with several days' worth of supplies and took off. With a shout, he gave the powerful stallion freedom to pick his own speed. As he knew he would, the horse took off like a bat out of hell.

They ran until both horse and rider were pushing their physical limits. Clint slowed the animal gradually until they walked to a stop. They were in the middle of nowhere, but it was his nowhere.

He unloaded and rubbed down Zeus, then set up camp for the night. As evening arrived, he lit a campfire. Darkness settled over the land and a disheartened mood settled over him.

He tried to explain it away as the aftermath of repeated counts of sexual frustration over the past few days, but under the uncompromising vastness of the heavens above, he admitted to a deeper hurt—the loss of the emotional ties that had been building between him and Skye. The way he'd been able to open up and tell her things he'd never told anyone before, the way she'd listened and the way she'd trusted him enough to share some of her inner feelings, too.

Skye's absurd story about him being the father of her little girl betrayed the reality of that bond.

He stared into the twilight sky, wishing for answers, wishing for comfort. Neither was in sight.

Skye parked her car in the shadows on the far side of the coffee shop. She wasn't ready to face Dawn, although she needed to get it together quickly because it was almost Dawn's bedtime and she had an overwhelming urge to be the one to tuck her in for the night.

"I've let you down, angel. Big time," she whispered.

Unlike yesterday's unloading in Clint's arms, tonight's pain was a cold emptiness that she knew couldn't be soothed by tears.

From somewhere, she dredged up the energy to get out of the car and head for the house. Luckily, there were only three wooden steps leading to the porch and a screen door to swing open.

"Mommy's back!" Dawn flew across the room and into her arms.

With a sudden burst of energy, Skye swept Dawn up for a hug. Over her shoulder, Skye's gaze met Chuck's. He glanced toward the doorway. When it remained empty, he looked to Skye once again. His unasked question hung in the air. Skye shook her head.

"Uncle Chuck took me out for ice cream. I got to have mine dipped in chocolate."

"Did you remember to say thank-you?"

"Yep."

"Good girl." She hugged Dawn close to her aching heart. "Ready for a bath and story?"

"Bubbles?"

"Sure."

Chuck came over and ruffled Dawn's hair. " 'Night, shortcake." He looked at Skye. "Are you coming back down to talk?"

"I'm exhausted. I think I'll call it a day, too."

"If you change your mind, I'll be tending bar with Beau until closing and then I'll be back here. Call if you need me."

"Thanks."

She knew she wouldn't want to talk about it, not right now, maybe not ever. But there was comfort in knowing someone was there for her if she did.

How could she even say the words out loud? How she'd ended her daughter's chance to have a relationship with her father and how she'd foolishly let herself believe there might be a happily-ever-after ending for her and Clint.

* * *

Clint was startled awake. He didn't remember feeling sleepy; in fact, the last thing he remembered was thinking he wasn't going to get any sleep tonight at all.

But he'd slept and he'd had that damned dream again! He opened his fly to give himself more space within the denim prison of his blue jeans.

How long was he going to have to put up with this? How long had he been putting up with it already? Six . . . almost seven years now.

He closed his eyes and found himself back in the middle of the dream. Terrific . . . now he was having it when he wasn't asleep!

The erotic content of the dream intrigued and enticed him to keep his eyes shut tight and watch as the fictitious events unfolded.

So real. It seemed so real.

Could something that seemed this genuine be just a dream?

In the darkest hours of the night, he allowed the ghost of an unthinkable idea to enter his mind. What if it hadn't been a dream . . . what if it had really happened? Teresa hadn't been with him that night, but what if some other woman had?

What if another woman had surrendered so sweetly to him and then sat back and watched him marry Teresa?

Impossible . . . wouldn't she have come forward and confronted him, demanded he marry her or at least try to blackmail him by threatening to tell Teresa about their erotic encounter? Or maybe she'd been as drunk as he was and didn't remember who she'd been with, or perhaps she'd been a professional who'd been cruising the parking lot and picked him up—except his wallet had been untouched.

The dream continued. He let it.

Its familiarity mocked him until it reached the point where the truck door started to open. He reached out as usual, but instead of fading to black, the scene sharpened as the interior lights flashed on. In the dream, he squinted at their brightness, but not before he'd gotten a look at the woman sliding out the door.

Love-tangled blond hair, kiss-swollen lips and blue eyes.

It was Skye.

He almost laughed out loud at the tricks his mind was playing on him now.

But look at the facts, pardner.

The dream had started about six years ago. Skye claims to have a five-year-old daughter. Was there a connection?

He had no proof either way that this was a dream or something that had really happened. First, he'd assumed it was a real event between him and Teresa. When he found out otherwise, he'd assumed it was a dream.

Once again, he considered the possibility he had made love that night with another woman.

And what if the other woman had been Skye?

Six

Clint stood on the Williamsons' front porch and waited for someone to answer his knock. He glanced at the swing he'd sat in with Skye the night before last. In the daylight, he could see it was in need of a coat of paint.

Daylight was real good at highlighting flaws. Most of the time...but rather than showing him the flaws in Skye's claim that he was her daughter's father, this morning's daylight made it seem more feasible.

The door opened. It was Skye's brother Chuck.

"'Mornin', Clint." His tone was polite, but his mouth was drawn in a tight line and his eyes were cold.

Clint nodded. "Chuck."

"I don't know if Skye's up yet. I'll check for you."

"I came to see the child." The child that might be his.

Chuck opened the screen door and stepped back to let him pass. "Dawn is in the kitchen having breakfast. The kitchen is through the living room to the right."

"Thanks."

Chuck nodded an acknowledgment. Clint headed for the kitchen, his boots clicking against the hard wood of the floor. As he neared a doorway, he heard the boiling gasp of an automatic drip coffeemaker finishing its cycle and a small, high-pitched voice humming.

Standing, looking into the kitchen, he spotted the source of the song immediately. A miniature version of Skye was looking into a half-full bowl of cereal, using her spoon to round up the cereal bits in the milk.

Ah, she looked like Skye, but her hair was different. Skye's was blonde, the girl's was dark.

About the color of yours, Slade.

He took a step into the room. At the sound, the child stopped humming and looked up, making eye contact.

The breath escaped from his lungs in a rush as he stared into her brown eyes. Eyes so much like the ones he saw everyday in the mirror that it couldn't be a coincidence.

"Hello, Dawn."

She smiled, it was Skye's smile. "Hi."

He made it to the table and sat before his knees had the chance to give out on him.

I have a daughter.

The truth of the situation crashed over him. He longed to grab hold of her and hug her to him, but he didn't want to frighten her. He watched her instead, completely in awe, as she went back to eating her breakfast.

"Clint is in the kitchen with Dawn." Chuck's words sent Skye's stomach and heart falling to her toes.

Not wanting to take the time to dress, Skye threw a robe over her nightgown and raced downstairs, pulling up short as she passed through the kitchen doorway. Clint was sitting at the end of the table, his back to her. The stiff line of his shoulders and rigid set of his spine signaled his tenseness. Dawn was sitting along the far side, in the chair closest to Clint.

"Good morning, Mommy."

Clint's back stiffened even more, but he didn't turn around.

"'Mornin', angel." Skye walked over and stood behind Dawn's chair. "Good morning, Clint."

"Skye." His voice was as emotionless as the look in his eyes.

Dawn leaned back and looked at her mother, smiling. Whatever she and Clint had been talking about hadn't upset or overly excited her, so Skye doubted Clint had said anything about being her father.

"Why don't you run upstairs, brush your teeth and make your bed?" Skye said to the little girl.

Dawn looked at Clint. "Will you still be here when I get back?"

"Yes, I will."

Dawn hopped out of her chair. "Good. I want to hear more about Zeus." She tore out of the room.

"My horse," Clint explained.

Skye wanted to rant and rave that she didn't care what his horse's name was, that all she was interested in was knowing why he was here. Why he had come if he was so sure she was lying to him last night. Instead, she spoke calmly and said, "Dawn loves horses."

"I guess maybe it's hereditary."

"You admit she might be yours. Last night you were sure she wasn't."

He shrugged. The sound of Dawn's footsteps echoed overhead.

Clint looked at the ceiling, then returned his gaze to Skye. "Has she ever asked about her father?"

"Yes."

"What have you told her about me?"

"Only that you live in Texas and that you're a cowboy. When she was little, cowboy was an easier concept for her to grasp than rancher."

His mouth was set in a tight line. "And what excuse did you give her for my absence?"

"She has friends whose parents are divorced, so she knows mommies and daddies don't always live together. Fortunately, she never asked for more details."

"Hopefully, my appearance now won't make her curious about my absence. I'd rather not have to try and explain why her mother has been lying to her."

Skye felt as if a bomb had exploded in her chest. She sat down in the chair Dawn had been using. "I didn't lie."

"Your telling her only that I'm a cowboy in Texas makes it seem like I chose not to see her. That I abandoned her. And that is a downright lie, lady." He stood, towering over her. "Why did you do it? Why did you keep my child away from me all these years?"

She was going to share Dawn with him, she didn't have to admit to her humiliation and vulnerability over being mistaken for Teresa.

The sound of small sneakers running downstairs kept Skye from answering.

Even though she'd been plagued with doubts ever since she'd told Clint about Dawn last night, she knew that Dawn probably would have started asking more questions about her father as she'd gotten older. And then Skye would either have had to lie or tell Dawn the truth about Clint. Now it didn't matter, she had started the ball in motion and there was no stopping it. She had to follow it through to the end. Regardless of where that end turned out to be.

"I'm back," Dawn announced. She climbed onto Skye's lap, facing Clint. "What happened after Zeus bit the trainer?"

"Would you like to meet Zeus?"

Dawn sat up straighter. "Could I?"

"If it's all right with your mother."

"Oh, Mommy, can we go?"

Skye wasn't sure Clint had meant to include her in the invitation, but she wasn't about to stand back and let him take Dawn. "All right."

* * *

Later that afternoon, Skye had to admit the day hadn't been total torture. As long as she kept her attention on Dawn and the child's excitement and delight at meeting all the ranch animals. The dude ranch had the same types of animals—cattle, horses, goats, chickens, dogs, barn cats. Even so, Dawn oohed and aahed over the Diamond S animals, especially Clint's stallion, Zeus.

Dawn was also awed by how much bigger everything was than at the dude ranch: the barn, the corrals, the mess hall, the bunkhouse.

After their tour, they had lunch on the patio at Clint's—entertainment was courtesy of the lively antics of several lizards.

Clint and Skye spoke to Dawn, but avoided talking to each other whenever possible, which was rarely necessary since Dawn kept up a rapid string of questions and exclamations about things she'd seen that morning.

"Wait till I tell everybody that I got to see real cowboy stuff," Dawn said. She paused, looking up at Clint. "You're a real cowboy, aren't you?"

"Yes."

"My daddy's a real cowboy, too."

Skye's heart dropped to her toes.

Clint looked her square in the eye. "Skye?"

She knew what he was asking. He wanted to tell Dawn that he was her father. For a moment, she wanted to say no. Once Dawn knew, there would be no turning back.

"If you're ready," Skye said.

He nodded, then turned to Dawn. "Dawn..." He cleared his throat. "Dawn, I'm your father."

Dawn looked to Skye, her eyes opened wide. "My daddy?"

Skye nodded. "Yes, angel."

Dawn jumped out of her chair and ran to Clint, hopping into his lap and throwing her arms around his neck. "Daddy, daddy. You're my daddy, the cowboy!"

The moment was bittersweet for Skye. Anything that brought such joy to her daughter's face brought a touch of joy to her.

After lunch, an elated Dawn was sent to have cookies and milk in the kitchen with Reina Flores, Clint's housekeeper. Clint led Skye into his office. A man, dressed in a western-style suit with an expensive-looking briefcase sitting by his feet, rose as they entered.

"My attorney, Miles Stokes. Miles, this is Skye Williamson, the child's mother." Clint walked behind the oversize desk and sat down. He looked every inch the rich, successful rancher he was. All business...no sign of doting father...or passionate lover.

Skye had thought she and Clint would handle the issue of Dawn between the two of them. The arrival of Clint's attorney proved she'd been wrong.

Miles pulled three stacks of papers from his briefcase. He handed one to Clint, one to Skye and kept the third for himself.

Several pages into the legalese, Skye was completely and totally lost. Quickly, she flipped through the rest of the pages, it didn't get any better.

"Excuse me. I think I should have an attorney here, too."

She didn't have an attorney. Had never needed one. There were a number of lawyers who were regular guests at the dude ranch. Surely one of them would be able to help her with this or recommend someone who could. Hopefully, the lawyer she found would let her pay the fee a little each month rather than needing payment up front.

Why did you get yourself into this? You could have been busy packing and heading for home today.

But then the vision of Dawn's face wreathed in smiles of excitement at meeting her father came to mind and Skye knew that despite her discomfort, this was the best thing for her daughter.

Clint pushed the telephone toward her. "Would you like to call him?"

"I...um. I'd like time to talk with him alone first, to explain the situation."

"So I'm not the last to know, after all."

She supposed he had a right to be bitter. "You're the first person I told. Chuck guessed."

Miles pulled a business card from his pocket and gave it to Skye. "Have your attorney call me and we'll set up an appointment for the four of us."

Skye glanced at the card. The law firm was in Houston. "All right." She hoped it wouldn't take her too long to find a lawyer.

"Ms. Williamson, if you wouldn't mind," Clint said. "Miles and I have some other business to attend to. Why don't you and Dawn go down to the stables? I'll join you there and we'll go riding when I'm done."

He didn't wait for her answer before turning to Miles. Skye left the room, closing the door behind her. She would do this for her little girl, and only for her.

Dawn rode with Clint on his black stallion, Zeus. Skye followed on a chestnut mare. Even though she lived around horses, it had been a while since she'd ridden one.

She tried to appreciate the beautiful scenery, but her attention kept drifting to the two on the horse ahead. They were chatting away like old friends. Too much distance was between her and them to be able to hear the conversation, but every now and then one of them would laugh and the sound floated back to her.

A knot of pain clenched in her chest. She felt totally shut off and alone. More alone than she did in the evenings, at their apartment, after Dawn had gone to bed.

You're doing this for Dawn.

The words fell into the rhythm of the horses' steps.

You're doing this for Dawn.

In the days that followed, they became a litany Skye repeated over and over again.

She was able to find a lawyer and arrangements for access were made. Fortunately, although Clint didn't bother to hide his dislike of her personally, his focus was "what would be best for Dawn," rather than "how best can I torment Skye."

Skye was comfortable with the arrangements made for splitting the rest of summer vacation evenly. But they were at a standoff over what would happen in the fall when it was time for school.

Clint wanted Dawn to live with him at the Diamond S and attend school in Harmony Ridge. Skye wanted her to stay with her. Neither was budging and the issue was headed for court.

How would she survive if Dawn went to live with Clint? Skye fought hard against worrying, knowing it would be too easy to succumb to complete despair. She focused all her efforts on getting through each day.

Word came from San Antonio that Lou Williamson was going to have bypass surgery. He'd asked to see all his children and grandchildren on Thursday, the day before the operation, including Chuck, Skye and Dawn.

Saturday, Skye would be going home to the Bar K Dude Ranch. Dawn would be going with her, but Clint would be picking her up in his plane in four days for the first of his visits.

This evening, Skye was getting a brief glimpse of what lay ahead. Clint had come to town to say good-bye to Dawn and ended up taking her for ice cream.

With the house all to herself, Skye had finished packing in no time. There were half a dozen other things she could attend to, but she ended up sitting in the living room where she had a clear view of the street.

Nervous wasn't usually in his vocabulary. But it came close to describing how he felt about being alone with his daughter for the first time.

You'd better get used to it, he told himself. If the judge rules in your favor, you'll have lots of time alone with her.

The problem was, the sum total of what he knew about five-year-olds could be written on a matchbook cover. Luckily, Dawn was real good at getting a conversation started and keeping it going. She had a comment or question about everything they passed on the way from the Williamson home to the Dairy Chalet.

The usual warm summer evening crowd was already there when they arrived, a mixture of families and teens in groups or pairs—no one he knew well enough that he would have to stop and talk.

Clint got into line with Dawn by his side.

"Do you know what you want?" he asked.

"A root-beer float."

"One of my favorites." He made a mental note to be sure root beer and vanilla ice cream made it onto Reina's grocery list before Dawn's visit.

Dawn smiled up at him. Automatically, he smiled back. He could hardly believe this cute-as-all-getout little girl was his flesh and blood.

The responsibility of it was monumental.

When they reached the window, Clint ordered two root-beer floats. He couldn't remember the last time he'd had one. They found a table in the shade.

"Are you looking forward to going home?" Clint asked.

Dawn shrugged. "I'm going to meet my granpa first. He's in the hospital."

"You have another grandpa and grandma who are looking forward to meeting you, too."

"Really?"

He nodded. "My dad and mom. They're up in Canada at the moment, but they're going to start heading this way."

"More granpas and granmas." Dawn spooned another bite of ice cream from the root beer. "I'm glad me and Mommy came here."

"Me, too, sweetie. Me, too."

A little more than an hour after they'd left, Clint and Dawn were back. Skye watched from behind the screen door as Clint helped Dawn out of the pickup, gave her a hug and kiss, then sent her up the walkway.

Dawn raced up the steps. "Mommy, Mommy, guess what? I got to see where you and Daddy went to school and one of my great-grandpas was the principal when they built the new building. It's not new anymore."

Skye smiled at her daughter. "That's nice, angel. Why don't you go inside and pick your bedtime story, I'd like to have a few words with your daddy."

As soon as the door closed behind Dawn, Skye raced to the street, reaching Clint's truck just as he was starting to leave.

Skye threw open the passenger door and hopped in. "Don't you dare try to hightail it out of here, you...you...I can't think of anything low enough to compare you to!"

"You wanted something, Ms. Williamson?"

"How dare you take Dawn to the elementary school."

"I didn't take her to the school. We drove by it on the way to get ice cream. Was I supposed to drive a mile out of my way to come in on the other side of town?"

"Of course not, but you didn't have to tell her what it was."

"She asked. Did you want me to lie to her?"

"It wouldn't have been lying just to say it was the school and not make such a big production out of it, including your family history."

He snapped his fingers. "That's right, you are the queen of lies of omission, aren't you? My most humble apologies, Your Majesty."

She refused to be drawn into that argument again. "You had no right to try and influence Dawn into wanting to stay here by showing her the school we went to...the school she could go to if she lived here."

"I didn't tell her that."

"She's smart enough, she could figure it out."

"What would be so bad about her going to school here? Her heritage is here and it's a damn good school."

"It's over a hundred miles between here and home."

"Your home."

"And Dawn's home."

"She can live with me. Or you could move back here. Get a house in town. I'm sure your parents would let you work for them."

Just what she needed, to move back to Harmony Ridge and live out her days as the mother of Clint Slade's illegitimate daughter. "I like where I'm living and I like my job."

"Then see Dawn on weekends during the school year."

"I work weekends." They had gone through all this with the attorneys, but Clint showed no signs of being flexible.

He shrugged. "The way I see it, that's your problem."

"I wish I had never told you about Dawn."

"Too late now." His smile was smug and tight. "If you're done spouting off, you can get out of my truck. I've got work waiting for me at home."

Skye was still seething, but knew Clint wasn't likely to budge on any issue. Her only option was to hope the court saw things her way.

Either that or disappear again . . .

Except how could she walk away from her family again? And how on earth would she explain it to Dawn?

Her thoughts were interrupted when Clint leaned in front of her to open the passenger door. His arm brushed across her breasts in the process.

Skye sucked in her breath. "I can open my own door."

Clint looked her in the eyes, only inches from her face. A shiver worked its way down her spine. As angry as she was with him, he still had the power to send her pulse racing and make her yearn to be swept into his arms. It was all she could do not to lean forward and join her lips with his.

"Then why didn't you open the door?"

"I was about to."

"Right." He moved away, settling into the driver's seat. "The door's open now. Use it."

Skye hopped out, slamming the door behind her.

Clint wandered out onto his patio. He tipped his hat back, rested his boot on the railing and watched the sun going down. He usually found the colorful desert show soothing. Not today. He was about as far from soothed as he could get.

He'd had a great time with Dawn and would have been fine if Skye hadn't come running out. Having her so close in the confines of his pickup had been torture. All he could think about was how it felt to kiss her. Her kisses were fresh in his memory, but there were also the vague dream-memories of making love to her.

He knew now that he really had made love to her, but he wondered how much of what he recalled in the dream was the real thing and how much had been embellished by his imagination over the years.

The only way he might be able to sort it out would be to make love to her again. He tried to convince himself that the idea was totally out of the question, but the rush of heat to his groin said otherwise.

The Williamson family rode in Alice's minivan and Beau's car to San Antonio. At the hospital, they gathered in the waiting room. Their mother met them there.

Hospital policy allowed only two visitors at a time. It was decided that Chuck and Skye would go first, then Dawn would change places with Chuck, followed by the rest of the family in pairs.

Skye took Chuck's hand as they walked slowly down the hallway until they reached their father's room. The door was open, but Chuck knocked twice before entering.

Small, frail . . . two words Skye had never associated with her father, were the first ones to flash into her mind when she saw him lying in the hospital bed surrounded by an assortment of beeping, blinking medical equipment and what seemed like miles of tubes and wires.

She carefully made her way to the side of the bed. "Hi, Daddy. How are you feeling?"

A glossy sheen of tears covered his eyes. "I've felt better."

Skye blinked back tears of her own, leaned over and placed a kiss on her father's forehead. As she straightened, Lou Williamson grasped her forearm and squeezed gently. "Thanks for coming, hon."

Skye nodded and backed away to let Chuck take her place. Pulling a tissue out of her purse, she wiped her eyes.

"Grab some chairs and make yourselves comfortable," Lou said.

It took some maneuvering, but soon Skye and Chuck were seated.

Lou started to speak then stopped to clear his throat. "I asked for you to come in case I don't make it through this operation. Don't want to leave without sayin' goodbye."

Chuck shifted in his seat and looked pale beneath his tan. Skye gave her brother's arm a reassuring squeeze.

Their father ran his hand across the stiff hospital sheet. "For a while there, during the heart attack, I wasn't sure I was going to make it. I got lucky that time. I hope my luck holds during this bypass procedure."

They sat quietly for a while, each lost in their own thoughts.

Lou broke the silence. "Did you bring the baby with you, Skye?"

"She's not a baby anymore, Dad. Dawn is five. She's with her cousins in the waiting room."

"All the regulars at the Rocking W send their best," Chuck said.

"In forty years I haven't missed work for more than two days in a row, until this." He waved his right hand toward the closest beeping machine.

"You'll be back at work before you know it," Skye said encouragingly.

Lou yawned. Skye and Chuck exchanged glances.

"Looks like I'd better send Dawn in while you're still awake," Chuck said, standing. The two men said their goodbyes with a grip on each other's arm.

Once they were alone, Lou asked, "How are things going, Skye?"

"Business is great. Everyone has been—"

"Your mother keeps me filled in on the business," he interrupted her. "I want to know how things are with you."

"Fine. Just fine." It was partly true. She had a roof over her head, a job she liked and her child was healthy and thriving. Was it selfish to want more from life?

At the sound of footsteps in the hallway, Skye looked up to see Chuck and Dawn. Chuck gave her a high sign. Skye walked across the room to take her daughter's hand and lead her to Lou's bedside. Once there, she lifted Dawn into her arms.

"Dawn, this is your grandpa."

Dawn's eyes were wide, her mouth a straight line until Lou smiled. Then she smiled back at him. "Hi, Granpa."

"Hi, Dawn."

Dawn patted his hand. "Sorry you don't feel so good."

"Thanks." Lou nodded his head as he looked at Dawn. "Except for her coloring, she looks a lot like you did as a little girl."

Skye wondered if Lou guessed Clint was Dawn's father. Sooner or later, the subject would come up between them. She didn't want her father to hear it through the grapevine. And once Dawn started visitations to the Diamond S, the vine would be buzzing with it.

Lou asked Dawn about school. With great seriousness, the little girl spoke of her kindergarten year. The two of them chatted until it was time for the next visitors to come in.

Skye kissed her father's cheek and lifted Dawn so she could do the same.

"'Bye, Granpa," Dawn said. "Get better."

"'Bye, Dawn. Watch out for the cows."

It was a warning Skye's father had always given his children when they'd parted—mostly in jest when they were young, more seriously once they were driving and the possibility of coming across loose livestock was real. Skye hoped and prayed this wouldn't be the first and last time Dawn heard the heartwarming words.

Seven

Skye and Dawn slipped back into their life at the dude ranch as comfortably as into a broken-in pair of blue jeans. With the warm companionship of her friends and co-workers, Skye was able to keep from dwelling on everything that had happened during her time in Harmony Ridge. Unfortunately, during the dark hours of night, nothing kept away memories of Clint's kisses and his touch on her bare skin.

Her mother called with the good news that the surgery had gone smoothly and Lou was recovering nicely.

Chuck stopped by the dude ranch on his way to his next rodeo and had dinner with Skye and Dawn. He managed to spark interest in more than one of the women he crossed paths with during his short visit.

Skye spent the next day fielding questions about him from her co-workers. They also got her to admit that she had another handsome, single brother back in Harmony Ridge.

All too soon the day arrived when Clint would be coming for Dawn. Skye packed the little girl's suitcase and fought back tears. Dawn was ecstatic about the chance to see her daddy again and fly in a plane for the first time.

Skye managed to hold it all together until the front door closed behind Clint and Dawn. As the sharp click echoed in the emptiness, her throat closed and her bottom lip began to quiver, a sheen of tears clouded her sight, but she continued to win the battle against letting them fall.

The sound of the door opening startled her. Straightening her back, she turned to see Clint in the doorway.

"Dawn says she forgot Snoopy."

Skye blinked back her tears, hoping he hadn't noticed them. "I'll get him."

She walked into Dawn's room and picked up the stuffed animal. Clutching it close, she turned. Clint was standing in the doorway, looking around the room. Skye imagined he had closets bigger than this.

"I would think you'd be glad for some time alone," Clint said.

Obviously she hadn't hidden her tears fast enough. "That just goes to show how much you know."

"Being rude isn't going to help."

Maybe not, but it made her feel better.

Skye shrugged. "Sorry."

They stood facing each other. Neither spoke.

Clint ran his hand over the back of his neck. "Whether we like it or not, our paths are going to cross a lot from here on out."

He was right. She hadn't thought much beyond the next few months, but looking into the future, she realized that there would be special events when Dawn would want participation from both her parents—school plays, graduations, a wedding, the arrival of grandchildren. An undeniable bond stretched between them. A bond that would exist even if one or both of them got married and had other children.

Always together, they would be Dawn's parents.

The thought of Clint married and having children with someone else didn't sound as appealing as she wished it would. After all, if he got busy with a new family, he might lose interest in Dawn and move out of their lives. But she couldn't wish that kind of heartbreak on her daughter. She was just going to have to buck up and learn to live with it.

"I guess for Dawn's sake we should try to get along."

Clint nodded. "Yes, we should."

He took a step and reached toward her. Her heart slammed hard in her chest. Was he going to take her in his arms? His hand was positioned more for a shake. But weren't they well beyond the handshake stage?

"I'd better get Snoopy to Dawn," he said.

You goof, Skye, she admonished herself. He's reaching for the toy.

She tried to make the handoff quickly, but ended up dropping the stuffed dog. They both stooped to get it. Clint's hand closed over hers. Warmth and sexual sparks flared where their skin made contact.

"She likes to snuggle him at night." Her voice sounded tight and forced.

He squeezed her hand gently. "I'll take good care of her, Skye."

"I know."

Dawn called every evening before bedtime. She sounded happy. Apparently, Clint had gone all out on having a bedroom and playroom decorated and filled for her. Not to mention buying her a pony, which she had named Princess.

Skye would have been worried that Dawn might not want to come home, if the little girl hadn't ended each conversation with messages to friends and animals at the dude ranch and an "I miss you, Mommy."

When Dawn's time at the Diamond S was up, Clint's housekeeper brought her back. By not showing up, Clint forced Skye to acknowledge that despite her best interests, she had been looking forward to seeing him again.

Clint left Zeus in the capable hands of one of the ranch hands and strode to the house. The sound of the front door closing seemed to echo through the house.

Today there were no racing footsteps and no call of "Daddy!" to welcome him home.

Dawn was on her way to her mother's. Their time together had seemed to fly.

He walked into his office. A box of crayons and stack of drawing paper sat on one end. Dawn had alternated between pretending to help him with his work and drawing pictures. Some of the drawings hung on his refrigerator and others she'd wanted to take to her "other home." He gathered the art supplies and tucked them into a drawer, for the time being.

She'll be back.

He knew she would, but even knowing that didn't soothe the dull ache or fill the emptiness inside him.

Much of his time was spent alone and mostly he was okay with it. When it got too bad, he'd head out into the wide-open spaces of the Diamond S. He'd just returned from a ride, but the little girl's absence had him feeling empty again. Empty and lonely. He understood why he'd found Skye in tears when he'd gone back for Dawn's stuffed dog.

Now, there's a subject to avoid completely... Skye.

He was able to avoid seeing Skye by sending Reina in the plane with Dawn, and he certainly didn't want to think about Skye, either. He didn't want to think about the tear-washed blue eyes and how much he'd wanted to pull her into his arms and hold her. Or how his insides had churned into knots when their hands had touched accidentally.

She looked all soft and innocent, but that was just cover for the conniving schemer who'd kept his daughter from him for six years. He'd missed so much. And if Lou Williamson hadn't had a heart attack, Clint probably still wouldn't know he'd fathered a child.

It made him angry enough to want to sue for full custody of Dawn.

A week later, Dawn's next scheduled visit to the Diamond S coincided with Lou Williamson's release from the hospital in San Antonio. Marge arranged a family picnic at the house to welcome him home, but as the day went on, more and more people wandered over from the bar and coffee shop. Lou held court from his recliner, which had been moved outside under the oak tree.

In the early evening, after dinner, Skye said her goodbyes and headed for Clint's to drop off Dawn before driving home. As soon as they arrived, Dawn insisted on going to the corral to check on her pony. Princess looked as happy to see Dawn as the little girl was to see her. After a final pat on the pony's nose, Dawn led the way to the house.

She started to open the door, but Skye stopped her. "We should knock or ring the doorbell, angel."

"Daddy said I didn't have to. He said this is my house."

"But it's not mine, so I need to ring the bell." She pushed the button.

Clint's housekeeper opened the door. "Miss Dawn." Reina welcomed Dawn with a hug. "And Miss Skye.

I'm so glad to hear your father is home from the hospital. Come in. Come in. Mr. Clint will be back anytime. Here, let me have the suitcase, I'll take it to Miss Dawn's room.''

"Could I take Mommy to see my room, Reina?"

"Sure, sweetie."

Skye couldn't help but be curious. ''I'll take the suitcase then,'' she said.

Dawn started off with a jump and a skip. Skye followed. Dawn led the way down several hallways until she stopped and opened a door.

"This is my room."

Skye walked through the doorway. The room was larger than their apartment. But what struck her hardest was the frilly, lacy canopied bed. It wasn't exactly like the room Skye had dreamed of having as a young girl, but it was close. It was definitely a room she wished she could have given her daughter.

Dawn pointed to a door on the left side of the room. "The bathroom is over there." She walked to the right wall and opened another door. "And the playroom is over here."

Dawn disappeared through the doorway before her sentence was finished. Skye set the suitcase by the dresser and followed. The playroom was smaller than the bedroom and it looked like Clint had robbed a toy store.

Dawn gave her a whirlwind tour. Skye was glad to see her daughter so happy, but the thought that there was no way she could compete with this when it came time to decide where Dawn would stay for the school year clung to her like a troublesome burr.

"Hey, where's my girl?" Clint's voice came from the bedroom.

Dawn took off like a shot. "Daddy!"

Skye walked to the doorway. Dawn was in Clint's arms, her own wrapped around his neck. The differences in their size made the child look smaller, like one of the fragile dolls sitting high on the playroom shelves.

Skye had a clear view of Clint's face. He was smiling, but it wasn't his usual smile. This one was warm and open. Seeing it tugged at something deep within her. The bond between father and daughter was clearly visible and already strong.

The moment his gaze met hers over their daughter's shoulder, the openness of his expression closed tight.

"Hello, Skye. I didn't realize you were here."

"My car's out front."

"I came in the back."

"Dawn wanted me to see her room," she said. It almost sounded like an apology... dang it all, she had a right to be here.

"What do you think?" he asked.

"It's lovely. You've really gone at this daddy thing heart, soul and wallet."

He raised one dark eyebrow. "I have lost time to make up for."

"Do you want to play blocks, Mommy?"

"No, sweetie, I need to be getting home."

Dawn's eyebrows pulled together in a frown. "Can't you stay? If you stayed, you *and* Daddy could tuck me in."

"Angel, remember how we talked about Mommy-time and Daddy-time? Well, tonight is Daddy-time."

"Daddy, can Mommy stay, please?"

Clint didn't look overjoyed, but he looked at Skye and said, "I figured Dawn would be tired out from the party today, so I thought we'd kick back and watch a video. You're welcome to join us."

"Please, Mommy. Daddy has lots of neat videos."

"If you're sure you don't mind," she said to Clint.

"Not at all." The tone of his assurance wasn't any more convincing than his invitation.

Clint headed for the kitchen to make popcorn. Dawn led Skye to the family room. There was a wide-screen TV and a whole shelf full of children's videos, most still in their wrappers. Dawn picked one.

Clint arrived with the popcorn, sodas and a pile of napkins. Obviously he'd already learned a thing or two about life with a five-year-old.

He and Skye ended up on opposite ends of the over-size leather couch. Dawn alternated between the two of them, and during the musical numbers got off the couch to dance.

Toward the end of the movie, Dawn settled into Clint's lap. "Mommy, come sit by me."

"I'm sitting over here right now, honey."

"I want you to hold my hand."

"Then come over here."

"I want to sit with Daddy, too."

Before she could answer, Clint spoke up. "Don't make such an issue out of it, Skye. Just move down here. I'm not going to bite."

Dawn giggled. Skye felt the blood rush to her cheeks. Surely they could sit side by side like two mature adults, even if they weren't the best of friends.

Not the best of friends? Boy, that was an understatement.

Clint probably couldn't wait for her to leave.

She slid the length of the couch until she could reach Dawn's hand. A small empty space was between her and Clint, but she swore she could feel heat radiating from him. Heat radiating and trying to draw her closer. It was hard not to give in to the temptation to snuggle against him the way she would if they were a real family spending the evening together.

A real family.

The words repeated themselves in her mind. Repeated and brought with them visions of how such an evening might end. Visions of closed doors, rumpled sheets and warm male. Lovemaking urgent and hurried, followed by patient and leisurely for as long as they could stand it, then fireworks again before settling down and holding each other as they slept.

She was torn from the erotic images by the ending of the movie.

When it was time to tuck Dawn in for the night, Skye stood on one side of the bed, Clint on the other. Clint kissed Dawn and Snoopy, then it was Skye's turn. She finished with a kiss on the stuffed animal's furry black nose, then stood. Her gaze drifted to Clint's mouth and her thoughts drifted to how incredible it felt to kiss and be kissed by him.

She told Dawn good-night and goodbye one more time and started to leave. Walking down the hall, she heard the click of Dawn's bedroom door as Clint closed it.

"Skye, wait." Clint reached her in several long strides. "If you've got a minute, I'd like to talk."

After the daydream she'd been having during the movie, she was looking forward to putting distance...a lot of distance...miles' worth...between them.

He led her to the living room and gestured for her to sit down. She chose one end of the couch. He took a wingbacked chair, leaning forward with his hands clasped between his knees.

"When and where was Dawn conceived?"

Skye was instantly on her guard. "You're not going to try to deny you're her father again, are you?"

He drew his shoulders back. "I'm not questioning that, I'm just trying to put together the pieces of what happened. I suspect it happened on a night when I'd been drinking heavily."

"It did."

"Where?"

She felt the blood rush to her cheeks. It was going to sound sleazy to admit out loud that their daughter had been conceived in a bar parking lot in the front seat of Clint's pickup.

"What do you want from me?" she asked. "Do you want me to admit the whole thing is all my fault?" He didn't answer. She looked at her hands clenched in her lap and continued, "All right, it's my fault. It happened in the Rocking W parking lot in your pickup. And yes, I knew better than to get into the truck with you, but I did it, anyway."

She glanced at him, expecting to see censure in his eyes. There wasn't any.

"Did you just walk over and hop into my truck un-invited or was there some enticement on my part?"

It was embarrassing how little enticement it had taken. His very existence was an enticement to her. "You offered me a kiss as a thank-you because I helped find your truck in the parking lot. I knew I shouldn't let you kiss me."

"Come on, Skye, you don't expect me to believe your parents were so strict they told you never to kiss a guy."

"Not someone I barely knew and certainly not the way you were going at it."

"I . . . uh . . . I didn't use force, did I?"

"Not at all."

He looked relieved.

"You didn't have to force me. From the first kiss, I was lost," Skye said. "No one had ever kissed me that way, and I liked it. I knew it was wrong to let a guy put his hands under my clothes, but you were there before I knew it, and it felt so good I didn't want you to stop.

I told myself I'd stop you soon, but things kept on going from there and I never did get around to pulling on the reins."

"I have some vague memories of the evening." He leaned back in his chair. His gaze grew more intense, as though he were trying to look through her eyes into her memory and see that night. "Was it your first time?"

She shifted, crossing her legs. "I'm not comfortable talking about this."

"Damn it, Skye, I was there."

"Then you should know the answer to your question."

"From what I remember, it seems to me that it was."

She was curious about what he remembered, but was reluctant to ask. "It was."

He ran his hands through his hair and swore darkly under his breath. "Did it hurt?"

"Of course."

"I'm sorry."

"Hey, it's not all your fault. Blame that one on Mother Nature."

"At least you're not holding on to the guilt for that as you seem to be for everything else," he said. "I can't help wondering why you don't lay some of the guilt on me, too. Heaven knows, I deserve it."

Skye looked at the toes of his boots. "It was dark, you were drunk. So drunk you don't even remember the . . . the incident."

"Do you want to know what I *do* remember?"

Eight

Skye nodded and raised her gaze to meet Clint's.

"I remember the softness of your skin, the way you quivered when I touched you, the way your nipples grew hard against my fingertips and even harder against my tongue."

Skye noticed she was taking short, shallow breaths. And when his gaze lowered to her breasts, she could feel the tightening that told her they were responding to his words the same way they'd responded to his touch that long-ago night.

His gaze dropped lower. "Also, I clearly remember the heat, the wetness, the soft moaning sounds and the breathless way you said my name."

He met her gaze and for long moments they looked into each other's eyes. Clint stood. Skye realized she wasn't the only one who'd been physically aroused by the remembrance of their lovemaking.

He held out his hand. She reached up, letting him draw her to her feet. Placing his hands along the sides of her neck, he used his thumbs to tilt her chin back. "I feel cheated because I can't remember everything about that night."

"You remember a lot more than I thought you did."

"Help me remember the rest." He spoke just above a whisper.

All Skye's senses were on overload. Logic said she should hightail it out of here as fast as humanly possible. But she knew she wouldn't.

She wanted to help Clint remember. Help him remember by making love with him again. Her reasons weren't purely charitable. Making love would give her relief from the yearning ache she felt throughout her body, most powerfully at the juncture of her thighs. That persistent ache kept getting stronger and harder to ignore every time Clint was near.

She reached her arms around his neck, urging him to kiss her. He complied with a fiery, hot kiss. A coming together driven by desires and needs stirred up by their discussion. Clint moved his arms around her waist, pulling her closer against him.

Oh, yes. No doubt about it, as she suspected from the glance she'd gotten of his blue jeans, the man was definitely aroused.

Skye spread her fingers wide and slid them up the back of his head, feeling the silkiness of his hair and pushing his parted lips even tighter against hers. The kiss went on and on.

Heavens, she had missed his kisses.

Clint pulled back, groaning. He buried his lips against the sensitive curve where her neck and shoulder met. "Don't kiss me like that unless you're prepared to let me keep right on going."

Her hopes for relief started to fade. "Prepared in what way?" she asked. "Like birth control or safe sex—prepared? I . . . I'm not."

He raised his head and looked at her intently. "I'm prepared for that part of it."

"Then I'm prepared for the rest."

A sexy smile curled his lips, sending a jolt of pure longing sizzling through Skye. Clint swept her up as if she were weightless. She rested her cheek against his rock-hard chest. Looking at the strong curve of his jawline up close, she could see traces of tomorrow morning's stubble starting to grow.

Tomorrow morning . . . Would she wake beside him, or in her own bed, alone as she always had?

Her thoughts turned to more immediate matters as Clint carried her through the double doors into his bedroom. Most of the room lay in shadow, but dim lights glowed from behind the headboard of the king-size bed, flowing across the earth-toned pillows and comforter.

He pushed the doors closed with his boot and continued into the room until they were just inside the circle of light. After a hard, fast kiss on her lips, he set her down in front of him, keeping one large hand spread on each of her hips.

Meeting his gaze, she noticed how in the dimness his brown eyes looked almost black. Only a faint glittery circle showed where the pupils began and ended. The increasing desire she saw there resonated with the physical yearning she was feeling. She shifted nervously from one foot to the other.

Slowly, he began undressing her, watching with rapt attention as more and more of her was uncovered. Skye was fascinated by the rise and fall of his chest as his breathing changed tempo.

When all she wore were panties, he started at her shoulders and brushed the tips of his fingers over her bare skin. He wove the sensual assault downward. Although the paths he drew down her body were narrow, every bit of her seemed to burn with the excitement of his touch. Reaching the elastic barrier, he teased along its edges until Skye thought she would scream with the frustration of wanting him to trail lower.

A soft moan escaped her throat. Clint slid his hands behind her, pulling her against him. Briefly, she registered the roughness of denim on bare skin, then she was totally consumed by the hard heat it was holding back. Going onto her tiptoes, tilting her hips and parting her thighs, she moved even closer, aligning their bodies as best she could with the layers of fabric still separating them. She arched her back, letting the tight tips of her breasts graze the fabric of his shirt, sending even more sparks through her.

Clint leaned her back even further, gaining access to the sensitive flesh along the side of her neck. He left a series of soft, wet kisses as he worked his way to her lips.

"How about helping me out of this shirt, darlin'?" he whispered against her lips. "And if I haven't busted through the jeans by the time you finish, I'd appreciate some help there, too."

He continued to kiss her, so she undressed him by touch until she needed to move so she could slide his jeans and briefs down. He slipped out of them and his boots and socks at the same time.

Skye caught her breath as she ran her gaze over him. Within the tight confines of his pickup, she hadn't seen much of his body last time they'd made love. He was an amazing specimen of male perfection. His body was well muscled from the physical work of running a ranch. The dim lights and the dusting of dark hair served to accentuate all she found fascinating.

Skye remembered vividly what it felt like to have him on top of her, sinking into her. Looking at him now, it was easy to understand why she had felt so full.

Glancing to his face, she saw he was watching her.

He ran one finger along the curve of her ear. "I guess you wouldn't be surprised to hear how much I want you."

"I want you, too, Clint."

He flashed her a heart-stopping smile. "I can't tell you how glad I am to hear that."

Taking her hand, he led her to the bed. While he opened the nightstand drawer to take care of protection, Skye pulled down the covers.

When they turned back to each other, Clint kissed her lightly on the lips. She started to reach her arms around his neck, but he stopped her by taking hold of her wrists. He drew both to the small of her back, holding them there with one hand.

Dropping to his knees, he kissed his way down until he reached the fabric obstruction of the last article of clothing. There he stayed until she quivered from the sensation. At the same time, he used his free hand to tease the sensitive skin on the inside of her leg, working from ankle to thigh. When he reached the top, he finally began to move the kisses lower.

As he continued downward, he nudged her panties out of his way until he could hook his finger around and slide them down her legs. His gaze worked its way up to meet hers. If she were made of ice, the heat in his eyes would have evaporated her right into steam.

"You're beautiful, Skye. More beautiful than I imagined."

With her watching, he slowly kissed her blond curls. His grip on her wrists loosened and he lowered her to the bed. Guiding one of her knees to each side of his waist, he leaned forward and continued kissing her where he'd left off. Her hips shifted as the ache within grew deeper and stronger.

He added his hands to the assault on her senses, spreading them over her hips, using his thumbs to sweep across the responsive skin of her belly. Skye rested her hands on top of his, feeling the subtle play of muscle as he moved.

"Love me, Clint."

As she heard the words, Skye realized they were more than a plea from her body for physical fulfillment. They were also a prayer from her heart.

Don't fall in love with this man, Skye. Loving him could only lead to heartbreak.

A seed of panic settled in her midsection. But it didn't have time to grow before Clint joined her on the bed. He moved them toward the middle of the mattress, drawing her into the circle of his arms.

Skye thought she might die from the pure pleasure of having his warm naked skin against her own.

Together they kissed, explored and reveled in the powerful sensations they were creating in each other. Skye settled onto her back, drawing him with her.

"Open for me, baby." Clint's voice was huskier than usual. His words faded into a growl as she complied and he sank himself into her.

Skye also cried out. It was so much better than she'd remembered. She lifted her hips to take him even deeper. He countered by pulling back, then pushing forward again and then again, setting them into the rhythmic dance between male and female.

He feathered his hands up her sides, finally settling one on either side of her head. He gazed at her, his eyes blazing with passion.

Skye closed her eyes as he lowered his mouth over hers. He drew his tongue across her lips, then entered her mouth in a sensual imitation of their lovemaking. She sunk deeper and deeper under the spell of his expertise.

A strange collection of sounds formed in the back of her throat, only to be buried in their kisses. Clint pulled his mouth from hers, burrowing into the soft skin beneath her ear. He increased the tempo of his strokes. Without his kiss to muffle her voice, the sharp cries and moans escaped.

"That's it. Sing for me, baby," he whispered.

He scattered hot kisses down the side of her neck, sliding lower until his lips touched, then closed around, one tight nipple. As he drew it into his mouth, Skye tightened her thighs around him, drawing him deeper and deeper, delighting in the joy of giving and taking intimate pleasures.

She continued singing to him with wordless music. He murmured incoherent messages in return. When his shoulders began to shake, she sensed he was nearing his climax. Poised on the brink herself, she didn't fall until he called out her name. Only then did she join him in an earth-shattering release.

"Skye, Skye." He repeated her name over and over again. She let the sound of it wash through her, healing old wounds of having him call out Teresa's name the first time they'd made love.

This time, he'd only made love to her. She was the woman in his arms and on his mind tonight.

Her eyelids drifted open and she met Clint's gaze. A calm peacefulness she'd never seen there glowed in his eyes. She brushed a strand of dark hair off his forehead, then settled her open palm against his cheek.

He turned his head and placed a kiss in the center of her palm. The simple touch set off a small set of quivers where their bodies were still joined. Clint responded by rocking his hips against her until the quivering subsided.

He rolled to the side, drawing her with him. Skye closed her eyes again, letting the warmth of his body and the satisfaction of their lovemaking lull her to sleep.

Skye woke gradually. It took only moments to realize where she was and all that had happened earlier. Clint was also awake. She started to smile at him, but something in his expression stopped her.

An intense expression was on his face and a haunted look was in his eyes. Skye started to speak, but he brought his mouth over hers, blocking off any words.

Hot kisses quickly led to more. There was a hard, fast almost desperate quality to their coming together this time. Clint was the driving source of the frantic pace, but Skye's body was a willing, eager participant, so willing she peaked more than once before Clint surrendered with her, calling out her name again.

Clint turned off the lights before he settled down with her in his arms. The darkness brought questions creeping up on Skye.

What now?

Where did they go from here?

She couldn't make herself ask him. She was afraid of the answers. He hadn't made any promises when he'd carried her to his bedroom, and she hadn't asked for any. If she had, they probably wouldn't have made love. Had it been a fair trade-off?

"Daddy."

Skye was sure that was Dawn's voice, but why was she calling her daddy? She pulled the covers off her head and looked up.

"Mommy?"

Skye came more fully awake. Looking around, she realized the sun was up, she was in Clint's bed and the shower was running in the bathroom. Careful to keep the sheet over herself, she sat up.

"Daddy has a big bed." Dawn hopped onto the side, bouncing. "Lots bigger than your couch bed. Daddy's really nice. Why didn't we come see him before?"

Skye wanted to crawl under the covers and not come out.

"It's a long story. Something we can talk about later." Maybe in twenty or thirty years....

"Amber's mommy and daddy sleep in the same bed every day. Are you going to sleep with my daddy every day? Does this mean you and Daddy are getting married?''

"No, we're not getting married."

"But why not? Don't you want to marry my daddy?"

She wanted to... for whatever that was worth.

"Your daddy hasn't asked me to marry him."

"But—"

"Good morning, Dawn."

Skye looked up to see Clint standing in the bathroom doorway. He was wearing a bathrobe and his hair was damp from the shower. How long had he been there? She'd been so focused on Dawn, she hadn't heard the water stop.

Dawn scooted away from Skye and went to Clint for a hug. "Mommy stayed overnight."

"I know, but she's leaving right after breakfast." He sent a pointed look in Skye's direction.

"Why can't she stay?"

Although Dawn had asked Clint, Skye answered, "I have to get back to work."

"Daddy, why can't Mommy work here, cooking for the real cowboys?''

"Why don't you go see what Reina is making for breakfast?''

Dawn drew her eyebrows down in a scowl, but set off to do as she was told.

Clint glared as Skye. "And you got all over me for letting her see the damn school." He strode to the side of the bed. "Letting her find you in my bed—"

"If you had locked the door, this wouldn't have happened!"

He put his hands on his hips. The top fold of the robe parted slightly, revealing a bit more of his chest. "All right, it's my door, I should have locked it. But where do you get off telling her that the only reason we're not getting married is because I haven't asked you?"

"I didn't say that was the *only* reason. It was just the first thing that came to mind. She woke me out of a deep sleep and I wasn't thinking clearly."

"Let's get one thing straight. I can't be seduced into a marriage proposal." He picked up the scattered clothing, tossing Skye's onto the bed in her general direction. "The sex was top-notch, but that doesn't mean I'm going shopping for an engagement ring today."

"Obviously you've forgotten that I was on my way to the front door last night when *you* asked me to stay." She gathered her clothes into her arms. "But just for the record, you don't have to worry that I might try to seduce a proposal out of you. There is no way I would marry a guy who had to be bribed, coerced or seduced into marriage. I prefer a man whose brain is in the vicinity of his hat, not his belt buckle."

She climbed out of bed as gracefully as she could under the circumstances and stalked into the bathroom, closing and locking the door behind her.

Clint and Dawn had a good day, for the most part. Other than those moments when Dawn would mention her mother. The "Mommy likes this" or "Mommy said that" burrowed under his skin.

As much as he loved his daughter and enjoyed her company, he was glad when her bedtime rolled around.

She yawned as Clint tucked the covers around her.

After snuggling deeper, she asked, "Do you think Mommy is pretty?"

"Yes, your mother is very pretty." Downright beautiful. Too beautiful for his peace of mind.

"Are you going to ask her to marry you?"

He wasn't surprised by the question. Although he'd expected it to come up earlier in the day. "You don't ask someone to marry you just because they're pretty."

"Why do people get married?"

That field of discussion could keep a roomful of grown-ups talking for hours. But what was the definitive answer to give a five-year-old?

"I guess most people get married because they love each other." He leaned over and kissed her forehead. "I'll see you in the morning."

"'Night, Daddy." She yawned, again. "I love you."

A sudden tightness gripped his chest. "I love you, too."

He walked to the door, flipped off the light and left the room, closing the door behind him. Maybe now he could get through an hour without having to think about Skye.

Fat chance. Especially when he walked into his bedroom. Would he ever be able to look at his bed again without picturing Skye in it?

Damn! He'd hoped that by making love to her, he could exorcise the haunting dream from his mind. But last night had been better than the dream, making things worse, giving him more and more details for the dream to draw from. Fully focused, mind-blowing details.

The original dream was a pale shadow compared to the passion between the two of them last night.

Having failed in his objective, he'd woken up grouchy. So he'd been out-of-sorts even before he'd found Dawn chatting with Skye on the bed. Because of his mood, he may have overreacted when he heard Skye telling Dawn they weren't getting married because he hadn't asked her.

He decided he'd rather not think about this morning. Last night had been a whole lot better...

He closed his eyes, picturing Skye standing naked in his arms. Her smooth stomach warm and quivering beneath his fingertips. Dawn, his child, had grown there. He bet Skye had been beautiful when she was pregnant. He wished he could have seen her with their child growing in her belly.

Their child...their flesh and blood...the miracle of life they had created. God, he hoped Dawn never found out her father had been drunk as a skunk and hadn't even realized who he'd been making love to....

For a moment, he let himself imagine what would happen if the condoms they'd used last night hadn't done their job. If Skye came to him carrying another child, he could watch the process this time, share the pregnancy, the birth.

Whoa, time out, pardner. You're way off the trail this time.

He'd gone into his first marriage after a night of extraordinary sex and that had been a disaster. No way would he make the same mistake again.

Having sex with Skye should have snapped his hormones back into control, but it hadn't. What was he going to do now?

Intellectually, he knew what he needed to do. He needed to look at Skye as nothing more than his daughter's mother and base their relationship on that. But it was hard to forget the way she felt in his arms and the way the two of them had been forming a relationship before Skye had broken the news of Dawn to him.

His thoughts turned to the little girl. Despite the changes Dawn brought to his life, he was glad for the chance to be with her. He would give her the moon if he could figure out how to get it down from the heavens.

One thought was bothering him, though. He hadn't liked being an only child. It had been lonely at times.

Someday, he'd like Dawn to have brothers and sisters. It seemed likely either he or Skye would get married and give them to her.

But try as he might, he couldn't envision any other woman in his bed except Skye, and the thought of her writhing beneath some other man made him want to plant his fist right in the nameless man's face.

* * *

"Hi, Mommy."

Dawn barreled into the dining-hall kitchen at the dude ranch. Skye had been expecting her. She'd heard the plane fly in. Glancing up, a smile on her face, expecting to see Reina, Skye was stunned to see Clint standing in the doorway.

Nine

Skye's heart sped up and a tingle of awareness swept over her nerve endings. All the man had to do was walk into a room and she was ready to fall into his arms. So what if they'd parted on an angry note last time they were together? So what if she had made a pledge never, ever to be in his arms again? He showed up and all her reservations and good intentions disappeared.

Clint nodded his greeting and politely acknowledged the introductions to her co-workers, who seemed to have appeared from all over the dining hall as if drawn by a magnet.

"Do you have a few minutes, Skye?"

She felt vulnerable and exposed. This was where she worked. It had been her home and her refuge for six years. Having Clint here felt strange. As though two separate parts of her life were colliding.

"Don't tell me. You'd like to talk, right?" Her tone was more acid than she'd intended.

Clint's eyes narrowed. His gaze pierced straight into her. The last time they'd sat down to talk, they'd ended up in Clint's bed.

Betty, the head cook, broke the awkward silence. "Everything here is under control. Why don't you go ahead and leave early today, get Dawn settled in?"

Without the excuse of work, Skye had no choice but to agree to talk with Clint. There would be no repeat of what had happened last time, but still her heart beat double time as she thought about the outcome of their last talk. The initial outcome—ending up in bed, not the final one—their argument.

On the way to their quarters, one of Dawn's friends ran up with the announcement of a new litter of kittens in the barn. The two little girls raced off to see the recent additions.

At first, Skye was unsettled by the thought of being alone in the apartment with Clint. But all things considered, it was probably best that Dawn not be in a position to overhear their conversation. With the possibility of her coming home at any moment, Clint would keep his distance.

Oh, sure, like he's going to touch you again when he suspects you would jump at the chance to lure him into a marriage he's dead set against.

Clint accepted Skye's offer of coffee. He took a seat at her kitchen table while she got the coffeemaker going. Once it was brewing, she leaned against the counter, crossing her arms over her chest.

With him seated and her standing, she was the one looking down, for a change, but it didn't put her at ease. She was too aware of him as a man, and also as an adversary in the battle for Dawn.

"How was your visit with Dawn?"

"It went well." He took off his hat and set it on the chair next to him. "My parents called. They plan to come to the ranch next time I have Dawn."

"I'm sure she's looking forward to meeting them."

"Dad reminded me that week is the Fourth of July. I don't know if you remember, but the Diamond S traditionally holds a barbecue on the fourth."

Skye remembered and her first thought was *how nice.* Growing up, she'd always loved the barbecues on the big ranches around Harmony Ridge. The annual Fourth of July bash at the Diamond S had always been one of the best. Lots of food, games, entertainment for all ages—Dawn would love it.

But then she realized that being at a barbecue at the Diamond S would thrust the little girl front and center into the local community.

She caught her bottom lip between her teeth, then released it with a sigh. "The whole town will be there..."

Clint shrugged. "We can rearrange her visitation days if you'd like. But that will only postpone the inevitable. She's met a number of the workers at the ranch and I'm sure word has already spread through town about her. Instead of letting the gossip fly, it might be best to face it head-on.''

''I don't want to point any fingers, but some of the residents of Harmony Ridge aren't going to be too tolerant about her being illegitimate.''

''That can't be helped. But presenting a united front will ease it somewhat.''

Did he expect her to be there? ''A united front?''

''You and I, and both sets of grandparents, if possible.''

Skye wasn't sure if Chuck had spread the word through her family that Clint was her daughter's father, or not. Even if he had, she would need to discuss being at the barbecue with her parents.

''I don't know if my parents would go. They're not that comfortable with my being an unwed mother.''

And was she comfortable enough with it to be there herself?

Being a single mom here in her new life was one thing, but going back to the town where she'd grown up, where people knew both her and Clint, was another matter. Everyone knew them, knew they'd never been married to each other, might even remember they'd never dated. But there they'd be in front of the whole town with living proof that they'd had sex.

The coffee was ready. Skye poured a mugful and set it in front of Clint. He thanked her, then took a sip.

"If your parents won't come," he said, "we can use your dad's health to explain their absence, as long as we can get some of the rest of your family—brothers, sisters, aunts and uncles—to be there."

"I'll see what I can do."

"I'm sure they'll cooperate if you tell them that it will be easier for Dawn to be accepted into the community if we all stand together. If you think it would help, I'll talk to them with you."

Skye shrugged. "I'll try first." Just in case her father decided a statute of limitations didn't exist on shotgun weddings. "There's another problem, though. Dawn doesn't really know what she's up against. She knows our situation is different from her friends' families, but she doesn't know the meaning of illegitimate, or the stigma some people impose on children whose parents weren't married."

Clint took a deep breath and let it out slowly. He frowned. "She's only five. Does she have to know?"

Skye wished Dawn never had to learn that particular truth, but how long could they keep it from her. "What if someone says something to her at the barbecue?"

"I can't believe anyone would be so crass."

"Probably not one of the grown-ups," Skye said, "but what if one of the kids repeats something they've heard their parents say? It's almost a given someone will pin the word *bastard* on her."

Clint's hands clenched into fists. "Then they'll have to answer to me."

"But should we do something to prepare her just in case?"

Did *forewarned is forearmed* work for five-year-olds?

He shook his head. "Anyone who has a real problem with it will probably get their message across by boycotting the barbecue."

"She's going to have to be told someday."

He was quiet for a while, then said, "I don't think it has to be yet."

"As long as no one else brings the subject to her attention, it might be easier to tell her when she reaches the age where she learns about boys and sex."

Clint raised one dark eyebrow. "When it comes time for that talk, I'll be sure she knows her daddy's got a big shotgun."

Skye looked at the floor. "So does mine."

"I guess I've managed to get my boot in my mouth this time. I'm sorry, Skye."

"I'm glad you're protective of her. It's just an all-around awkward situation." She returned her gaze to Clint. "It's going to be hard knowing what to tell her when the time comes. I don't want her to feel bad about herself, but I want to protect her from making the same mistake I did."

He wrapped his hands around his coffee mug. "It doesn't seem right calling a sweet little thing like Dawn a mistake."

"The same thought crossed my mind the first time I held her in my arms."

"It's hard for me to imagine her as a baby. I'd like to see her baby pictures sometime."

"I still have the negatives. I could have some made for you."

"I'd like that. Thanks." He took a sip of coffee. "Let me know how much it costs and I'll pay you back. I'm sure my mother would appreciate having some copies, too."

None of her family had said anything, but Skye was sure they would enjoy seeing them, too. "I'll start going through them tonight."

"Would it be too much trouble for me to see a few now?"

"No. Not at all."

Skye went to the hall closet and collected the two photo albums that held the pictures taken since Dawn was born.

The first few pages were shots Skye's friends had taken of her getting ready to leave for the hospital—front view and side views. When she would have flipped past them quickly, Clint stopped her. Leaving the albums with him, she walked around to the other side of the table and sat down.

His face was free of emotion, but the amount of time he spent looking at the pictures of her, belly rounded with their baby, seemed to suggest he wasn't as unmoved as he appeared.

What was he thinking? Skye wished she could read minds.

Finally, he turned the page. Dawn's first picture was there, along with a lock of her hair and copies of the footprints from her birth certificate.

A faint smile curved the corners of Clint's mouth. "Such tiny feet."

Despite the ache in her heart at the wall between herself and Clint, Skye couldn't hold back a smile at the wonder in his voice. In her mind, she pictured him holding a baby in his arms... their baby, but it wasn't Dawn.

Stop torturing yourself this way.

Clint had made it clear there was no future for them beyond their parental roles in Dawn's life. There would be no other babies for the two of them together.

"You look tired. Was it a long labor?"

Skye glanced at the picture Clint was looking at. She looked as though she'd just run a marathon—exhausted, but triumphant. "It took about twenty hours."

"How was it?"

"It lives up to its name. But once they put the baby in your arms, it all seems worth it."

The muscles in his shoulders and along his jaw tightened. He looked at her, his eyes cold. "That's what you stole from me. The chance to hold my baby in my arms."

The force of his anger sucked the breath from her lungs. "I'm sorry," she whispered.

"There's no way I can forgive you for that."

She tried to swallow past the lump in her throat and bit her tongue to keep from repeating she was sorry. If she could only go back to when she'd been expecting and do things differently...but who could say how that would have worked out?

He might have offered to marry her, but that was no guarantee the marriage would have succeeded. Clint might have pined for Teresa and resented Skye for coming between them. They could have divorced and ended up sharing Dawn the way they were now, anyway. But Clint and Dawn would have had each other from the beginning, would have formed a bond early on and not have had to wait until Dawn was five. So many possibilities.

It didn't seem fair that at twenty, she'd been forced to make a decision that had had such an impact on so many lives. She hadn't been old enough, or wise enough, but the decision had been hers to make.

If Clint hadn't called out Teresa's name that night of their lovemaking, she might have chosen differently...then again, maybe not. Would she have been able to find the courage to walk up to Clint back then and tell him she was pregnant? It had taken every last ounce she could muster to approach him that night in the parking lot with an offer of coffee.

"What if I had come to you back then and told you I was expecting?"

"I would have married you."

"But you were engaged to Teresa."

"I would have broken the engagement. I wouldn't have shirked my responsibilities."

She wondered if he would have questioned whether the baby was his, but she was bothered by another question whose answer seemed more important.

"As much as you loved Teresa, would we have had a chance at making a marriage work?"

A strange look crossed his face. "It's useless to talk about what I might have done or whether things would have worked out. I was never given a choice." He slammed the photo album shut and stood. "I'll call you next week about the barbecue."

The next morning at work, everyone had to get in their two cents' worth about Clint. Skye did her best to respond good-naturedly, but it took a toll.

Betty came back to the apartment with her. Skye wasn't surprised when the other woman managed to bring Clint into the conversation.

"He's a real looker and he obviously has bucks if he has his own plane," Betty said. "Have you considered snatching up this guy?"

"The whole situation is a tangled mess."

"Is he married?"

"Divorced."

"Is he dating anyone seriously?"

Skye realized she didn't know the answer. Other than the rumors about a woman in Dallas that Alice had mentioned, she had no idea. Could he be involved with someone? Would he have a date with him at the bar-becue?

"I don't think so, but I haven't asked him about his love life."

You let him carry you off to his bed, but didn't know if he was spoken for already.

Would he have made love to her if he were in a seri-ous relationship?

"I say, whether he is or not, you set that boy down, get the mess untangled and work things out between the two of you."

Betty made it sound so simple, but she didn't know Clint. His words and his biting tone were clear in Skye's mind...*there's no way I can forgive you for that.*

"It would be easier to stop a stampede than to work things out with Clint."

Betty patted her hand. "Now, don't be so negative. Have you told him you love him?"

Love him?

Her first response was to flat out deny it, but then she realized she couldn't and be honest with herself. How? Why? The idea had teased the edges of her thoughts when she'd asked him to love her the other night, but thinking about it afterward, she'd pretty much dis-missed it as heat-of-passion stuff.

She'd had a crush on him before and the sexual chemistry between them was explosive, but that wasn't love. Pictures started to flash through her mind: the way he'd held and comforted her as she'd cried, the way he was so kind and gentle with Dawn, the love and longing on his face when he'd looked at Dawn's baby pictures.

Betty was right. She did love him ... Lord help her.

Holidays were a busy time at the dude ranch. But given the circumstances, Skye was able to get time off to attend the Fourth of July barbecue at the Diamond S. She also took tomorrow and the next day off so she could go to Harmony Ridge and talk to her parents. It seemed best to speak to them in person.

Chuck hadn't told them Clint was Dawn's father, but word that Skye and Dawn had been out at the Diamond S and also that Dawn had been there on her own had made them suspect Clint was their granddaughter's father.

They seemed to take the news calmly... her father made no mention of his shotgun. And although Skye sensed they were still uncomfortable with the way things stood, they agreed to go to the barbecue, for Dawn's sake.

Before leaving, Skye spent a few minutes alone with her mother.

Marge looked at her youngest child, with sadness in her eyes. "Is there any chance the two of you might get back together?"

"See, that's part of the problem, Mom, we never were together in the sense you mean."

"Still—"

"Clint is angry I didn't tell him when I found out I was pregnant. I kept him from sharing in Dawn's early life. He'll never forgive me."

"Why didn't you tell him, dear?"

"He was engaged."

"But he wasn't married yet."

It sounded so easy and logical when everyone else said it. Why hadn't it felt that way back then?

"I can't keep going over it and over it. I need to put it behind me, get on with my life and help Dawn get on with hers."

Marge nodded her understanding. "Well, your father and I will be at the barbecue to help you."

Skye prayed for rain. Even though she knew bad weather would only postpone the inevitable.

Preparations were well under way at the Diamond S when Skye and Dawn arrived. The bandstand, tables, games and parking areas were being set up on the far side of the barn, out in the open away from the workings of the ranch, even farther from the ranch house.

When they reached the house, Skye saw a large motor home parked in the driveway.

"Daddy said my other granma and granpa have a house on wheels. Is that it?"

"I don't know for sure, but it probably is."

Skye got Dawn's suitcase out of the trunk and they headed to the front door. Skye rang the bell, then smoothed her hand down her denim skirt. She'd chosen it hoping it would keep her cooler than blue jeans.

She questioned her choice though when, after warmly greeting his daughter, Clint helped himself to a long perusal of her bare legs.

"I'll put Dawn's suitcase in her room," she said finally.

Clint took Dawn's hand. "Join us on the patio when you're done."

As a rebellious payback for his bold look at her legs, she let her gaze wander over his retreating back. Most of his dark hair was hidden beneath his cowboy hat. His broad shoulders and trim waistline were covered by a black western shirt and his enticing backside and long legs were set off to perfection by black jeans.

Some revenge, Skye. The only one suffering here is you.

Suffering because Clint and his to-die-for buns were off limits...

With a sigh, she headed for Dawn's room. She left both the suitcase and her purse on the little girl's bed.

There was no denying she was nervous about seeing Clint's parents. She knew them by sight from around town and had waited on them in the coffee shop a few times, but that was all. As she remembered them, Jack Slade was an older version of his son and Hope was a petite, dark-haired woman.

As Skye neared the patio, she heard Dawn's voice. "What did the farmer say after he lost his tractor?"

A male voice she assumed to be Clint's father answered, "I don't know. What did the farmer say after he lost his tractor?"

Skye reached the doorway and saw Dawn perched on Jack's knee, looking up at him with a wide smile on her face.

Dawn giggled then said, "Where's my tractor?"

Mr. and Mrs. Slade and Clint all laughed. Obviously it hadn't taken Dawn long to charm Clint's parents. Skye almost hated to interrupt the happy group.

Hope glanced over and spotted her. She stood and crossed the patio. "Skye, honey, come sit down." After a brief but warm hug, the older woman led her to a chair.

Jack nodded in her direction. "Nice to see you again, Skye."

Reina arrived with a tray of iced tea and lemonade. Dawn continued holding center stage as Jack and Hope asked her question after question, getting to know their first grandchild.

Skye's attention kept drifting to Clint. He seemed preoccupied. Maybe he wasn't looking forward to this any more than she was....

When it was almost time for the guests to arrive, they went out to the picnic grounds. It didn't take long for the place to start filling up.

Skye saw old classmates from school, former teachers and former customers. Everyone was polite, but there was a definite feeling of separateness. Whether it was because word was out about Dawn, or because she no longer lived in town, she didn't know. Fortunately, at least one of her family members managed to be near her most of the time.

Although no one brought up the subject of Clint to her, she heard bits and pieces of conversations, including talk of the night she and Clint had gone dancing together at the Rocking W.

Every time his name was mentioned, she found herself seeking him out in the crowd. His height helped her spot him. As she remembered from years past, there always seemed to be a number of females hanging around him.

Did you expect that would have changed? Reality check, honey.

Of all the men in the world, why did she have to fall in love with this one?

Occasionally when she sought him out, he would be looking at her. Other times while she was watching him, he would turn and look at her, almost as though he'd sensed her watching him. Anytime their gazes met, she felt a jolt of desire and longing.

Right before the barbecue was served, Jack Slade took Dawn onto the bandstand. He welcomed everyone, introduced Dawn and let her say grace before leading her to the front of the food line.

As afternoon turned into evening and a considerable dent had been made in the beer supply, Skye noticed some of the men giving her covert glances, others staring boldly. She began to feel downright uncomfortable.

Surely she'd put in enough time. Quietly, she said her goodbyes to her family and Dawn, then headed to the house to get her purse.

On her way back down the hallway, she noticed an open door to the right. If she remembered correctly, it was Clint's office. She could have sworn all the doors were closed when she'd walked past them only minutes before. Walking slower, she approached the door.

Clint was standing just inside the room. "Leaving without saying goodbye?"

Ten

———

"**I** didn't want to interrupt your conversation with your harem."

Clint smiled smugly. "Jealous, Skye?"

"Not on your life."

She started down the hall, but stopped when Clint took hold of her arm and drew her into the office. He closed the door, locked it, then moved toward her until she was backed against it.

"If you weren't jealous," he said, "I don't think you would have noticed who I was talking to."

He had a point, but she wasn't about to admit it. "You're hard to miss in a crowd."

"Why, darlin', is that a compliment?"

"No. A statement of fact. You're tall and dressed all in black."

Reaching out, he fingered a strand of her hair. "I don't have trouble finding you in a crowd, either. I just look for hair the color of sunshine."

"My sisters' hair is almost the same color."

"Almost, but not quite."

He moved closer until they were almost touching. Raising his arms, he rested one hand on each side of her.

What were they talking about?

Lord, it was hard to think with him so close.

Skye brought her hands up, placing them on the rock-hard wall of his chest. She meant to push him back a bit, gain some thinking room, but instead she moved them over the front of his shirt. Feeling. Remembering.

He leaned forward and covered her mouth with his, devouring, igniting her passion instantly. Reluctantly, she admitted to herself, this was exactly what she had wanted from the moment she'd arrived at the Diamond S today. It was the reason she hadn't been able to keep her mind or her gaze off him.

It took little more than a few tugs to unsnap the buttons on his shirt and gain access to his warm, hair-roughened skin. Her fingers grazed across dark nipples that pulled into hard nubs as she teased them.

He quivered from her touch. The reaction made her bolder, and she moved her fingers lower. His muscles tightened even more as he sucked in his breath.

In imitation of the way he'd loved her the other night, she drew her mouth from his and began to trail kisses down his body. By the time she lowered herself to her knees, she had him freed from his jeans. His sensitive flesh was hot against her palm, lips and tongue.

He groaned deep in his chest, threading his fingers through her hair. His hands were trembling. A sense of feminine power shot through her.

She ran one hand up the back of his leg, feeling the tension in his muscles. A little farther put her in touch with the part of his anatomy she'd admired as he'd walked away from her earlier in the day. His backside felt as good as it looked.

Did you have any doubts that it would?

He slid his hands beneath her arms and drew her to her feet. Reaching under her denim skirt, he took a firm grip on her panties and pulled them off as he lifted her.

Skye wrapped her arms around his neck and her legs around his waist. Her back came up hard against the door and Clint lowered her over him, entering smoothly and deeply. They both cried out.

His hands were hot against her bottom, holding her in place. He captured her mouth in a thorough kiss. Clint set a much slower tempo for their lovemaking this time, drawing every drop of sensation out of each thrust and retreat.

A niggling doubt tried to invade Skye's thoughts. They really shouldn't be doing this, not at all and especially not here and now with the whole town of Harmony Ridge outside.

"Clint, what if someone notices we're both missing?" she asked breathlessly.

He gave her a pained look. "You want me to stop?"

That was the last thing she wanted. "No."

"Then relax and enjoy it."

He was right. Since it was already happening, she might as well enjoy it, savor it.

She let her worries drift away and focused on Clint and the phenomenal sensations he was creating in her. From her position, it was difficult for her to move. But she did what she could, circling her hips and rocking against him.

He widened his stance, bracing them more securely for the inevitable shock waves that were approaching quickly. Their cries of triumph became part of their kiss. The cries faded, but the kiss lingered as though they were trying to hold on to the magic for as long as possible.

Skye was only vaguely aware of being lowered to her feet. Her legs were as wobbly as those of a newborn colt, but luckily Clint and the door kept her from falling. She kept her eyes closed, listening to the harsh sounds of their ragged breathing.

"Skye?"

"Hmm?"

Clint chuckled.

Skye opened her eyes and looked at him.

"What kind of spell do you have over me, Skye?"

"The same one you've got over me."

He rubbed his thumb across her bottom lip. "Can I ask you a personal question?"

Skye shrugged. After the physical intimacy they'd shared, how much more personal could his question be? "I guess."

"Is sex always like this for you?"

She caught her bottom lip with her teeth. A simple yes would answer the question honestly. Clint was the only man she'd made love with, and each time they'd come together had been earth-shattering. She was tempted to say yes and let it go at that, but figured it would fall into the lie-of-omission category Clint had put her in. And if even the slightest chance existed for them as a couple, she knew complete honesty would be essential from here on out.

But how would he feel knowing he'd been her only lover? Heaven knew, his ego didn't need any more feeding after the women of Harmony Ridge had been chasing him all day long.

"You...you're the only man I've ever made love with."

He looked stunned, as if she'd emptied a pitcher of iced tea over his head.

He gave a long low whistle. "You're pulling my leg, right?"

"No, I'm not."

"You're very good at it."

"I had a good teacher."

He looked skeptical. "I'd love to take all the credit, but I can't."

She feathered her fingertips across the nape of his neck. "I guess you bring out the best in me."

The corners of his lips curved upward. "And you seem to bring out the worst in me. Believe me, when I followed you up here, I didn't have any intention of making love to you."

"I believe you. That night six years ago, at the Rocking W, when I walked up to you, I didn't have any intention of making love with you, either."

"Why did you walk up to me?"

Skye hesitated again, but after a moment decided he might as well know this, too. "I had a crush on you and I thought it was my big chance to get you to notice me."

His eyes opened wide. "You had a crush on me?"

"Along with just about every other female in Harmony Ridge." She shrugged. "My plan to get your attention backfired. The next night at the church picnic, you announced your engagement to Teresa."

At the mention of his ex-wife's name, a shutter seemed to close over his emotions. Despite his statements to the contrary, Skye wondered if he was still in love with the other woman.

He moved away from her, turning his back to button his shirt and adjust his jeans. Skye located her panties on the floor and slipped them on. Her hands were shaking, so she had a much harder time getting them on than Clint had had taking them off.

When she looked up, she found Clint standing in front of his desk, his hands clenched into fists pressed against the dark wood.

She knew she should leave now, but he'd brought up the subject of their first night together and there were thoughts and feelings deep within her that wanted out.

"The other night when you asked me to help you remember the night we made love, we...um...we covered most of what there was to remember, but there was a difference."

"Obviously. You weren't a virgin."

"Besides that." Skye struggled to find the words to tell him what she'd never told another soul. "The first time...at the end...you called me Teresa. 'I love you, Teresa.' You said it over and over until you fell asleep."

He ran one hand through his hair and across the back of his neck, before returning to his original position. Although he didn't speak, the tension in his muscles spoke volumes.

Skye continued, "You were so gentle, so understanding about it being the first time and all. But when you called out her name, I realized that all the loving tenderness, warmth and caring had been for her, not me. I was so ashamed and embarrassed by what had happened. I was young, naive, still believing in true love and happily-ever-afters. I never would have tried to come between a couple in love, but I didn't realize how much you loved her until after we'd made love."

She took a deep breath, fighting against the tightening in her chest, struggling to keep her voice sounding normal. "When I found out I was pregnant, I didn't have the heart to try and break up your engagement. Besides, if I'd succeeded, I wouldn't have had the courage to spend the rest of my life with a man who was in love with someone else. That's why I didn't tell you I was pregnant. Looking back at how short your marriage was, it seems I made the wrong choice, but believe me, I had the very best of intentions. I thought if I came forward and you married me, both you and Teresa would be miserable, and by leaving, it would just be me.''

She wanted to ask what he was thinking, but was afraid to hear the answer.

''I'm not asking you to forgive me,'' she said, ''but I wanted you to know why I made the choices I did. Despite the way things have turned out, I was trying to do the best I could.''

She was afraid if she stayed any longer, she would end up telling him she loved him.

''I guess I'll be going now,'' she said.

''I'll have Reina bring Dawn home on Wednesday.''

It was painfully clear how he felt about her confession. She hadn't asked for forgiveness, but she'd been hoping to receive it . . . the hope was as empty as her heart.

Skye let herself out of the office, made her way to her car and headed for home.

But how could she be going home, when her daughter and the man she loved were behind her?

Long after he heard the sound of her car drive away, Clint remained in his office.

He'd been her only lover. He wanted to believe it didn't matter, but he couldn't quite convince himself.

From the moment she'd arrived at the Diamond S this afternoon, he'd been fighting against an almost primitive awareness of her. Every time she'd looked in his direction, the awareness had increased, so that when he'd seen her leave for the house it had been impossible for him not to follow.

As he'd waited for her to come past his office, he'd thought about what he wanted to say to her—how he was proud of how she'd handled herself in what must have been a difficult situation for her and how proud he was of their daughter and what a good job she'd done raising her. All his carefully thought-out words had flown from his mind the minute she'd come into view.

He was used to being very much in control, and these uncontrollable urges he got around her were totally perplexing.

The admissions she'd made were equally as startling and even more unsettling . . . the reasons she'd kept her pregnancy secret.

She was convinced he would have been unhappy being married to her. The irony wasn't lost on him. He thought he'd made love to and fallen in love with Teresa, when he'd actually made love to and fallen in love with Skye.

His heart went out to Skye. Missing Dawn's early years had hurt him, but Skye had done it for him, because she believed he was in love with Teresa. She'd had a crush on him, yet she'd let him go. Not to mention that she'd walked away from the chance to marry into the richest family in the county—and she'd done it for him.

So he could be happy.

And he'd ended up lonely and miserable.

His muscles had ached from the effort it had taken to keep from going to her and gathering her into his arms as she'd made her confessions. God, he'd wanted to comfort her. But how could he when he was the cause of her torment?

He couldn't stand to think about it. But as much as he wanted to hop on Zeus and head out on the range to think and clear his mind, he couldn't. He needed to get back to the barbecue.

The questioning look on his father's face made him suspect that Jack had noticed he and Skye had disappeared in the same direction at about the same time. He hoped no one else had noticed. Skye had asked about it, but by that time, he'd been way beyond the point where he cared about anything except the woman in his arms.

Not ready to deal with his father's questions, Clint moved in the other direction. He made his way to the bar and grabbed a beer. He didn't drink much these days, but right now he needed a long cold one.

As usual, a small cluster of men were gathered nearby, so they wouldn't have far to go for refills. Clint nodded in response to their greeting.

As he started to walk past, one of the men, Walt Harper, stopped him. " 'Fess up, Slade. What's it like ridin' Skye? I'll bet she's some kind of wild.''

Clint's beer hit the dust and he grabbed hold of the man's shirt, pulling him up until they were eye level. "That's my daughter's mother you're talking about. And I'll thank you to keep some respect in your tone.''

"How much respect are you showin' by not even marryin' her?''

"That's between me and Skye and isn't any of your damned business." He let go of Walt and took a step back. Looking around, he noticed how much attention they'd drawn. "And that goes for the rest of you, too.''

He grabbed another beer and headed toward the horseshoe pit.

Clint went through the motions the rest of the evening. He was grateful when a sleepy Dawn finally admitted she was ready to call it a day.

Once he had her tucked in, he went into his office. He sat in the leather chair behind his desk and stared at the door, remembering and reliving the events that had taken place against it earlier.

Walt Harper's words about respect and marriage haunted him. He'd wanted to slam his fist into the other man's grinning drunken face, but it hadn't seemed fair to hit a man for telling the truth. Except what he'd said in reply was equally as true—the matter wasn't anybody's business except his and Skye's.

He was still there when his father opened the door. "Mind if I come in?''

"Be my guest."

"You did a good job of handling Walt," he said as he took a seat across the desk from Clint.

Clint grunted noncommittally.

"Beau and Lou Williamson were chomping at the bit to get in on the action, too."

"They heard?"

"Son, a lot of people heard."

He swore darkly.

Of course, it was likely Beau and Lou would have gotten into the action on Walt's side of the argument. He could understand that. If he ever found himself in a similar situation with Dawn, he'd want to wring the guy's neck. The thought snuck up on him, but it hit with more force than any opponent he'd ever met in a fistfight.

God, he felt like a real lowlife.

Jack leaned forward in his chair. "I know it's none of my business, either, and I don't know what went wrong between the two of you when you were younger, but can't you and Skye patch things up, for Dawn's sake?"

How could he explain there had never been anything to patch up?

He wondered what Skye would say, though, if he suggested they try to be together for Dawn. She might agree, but the idea didn't appeal to him. He'd married once for the wrong reasons. If he ever got married again, it would be because he and his bride were in love with each other—really in love with each other.

"Dad, I appreciate your concern, but you're right, it isn't any of your business."

"You know everybody makes mistakes now and then," his father said, seemingly undaunted. "Part of what has helped your mother and I stay together so long is knowing when to say I'm sorry and being big enough to say I forgive you, even when you're still hurting."

"She kept my child from me, Dad. I missed five years of Dawn's life."

But she did it so you could have Teresa.

"You're not the only one who missed out on Dawn. So did your mother and I, along with Lou, Marge and the other Williamsons. But we've got her in our lives now and what we need to focus on is the future." His father stood. "If you and Skye need some time alone, your mother and I would be glad to watch Dawn."

"Thanks for the offer."

"I know you had a bad experience in your marriage with Teresa—"

"Dad," Clint interrupted.

Jack smiled. "None of my business?"

"Right."

"Okay. Guess I'll call it a night."

"See you in the morning."

Shortly after his father left, Clint turned out the lights and headed for his empty bed.

When Skye arrived at the dude ranch, she was exhausted. She almost wished she'd accepted her parents' invitation to spend the night, but she'd felt it best to come home. If she'd been close to the Diamond S, she might have been tempted to see Clint again.

She'd come too close to admitting she loved him. Once she did that, she'd probably lose all pride and beg him to forgive her, beg him to love her in return.

She entered her apartment and noticed the message light on her answering machine blinking. It was Heather. She wanted her to call as soon as she got in, no matter how late it was.

Dawn? Dad?

She dialed her sister's house.

"Heather, it's Skye. Are Dawn and Dad all right?"

"Yes, they're fine."

"Thank God."

"Gee, I'm sorry, Skye. I didn't mean to scare you. I should have mentioned on the machine that it wasn't an emergency."

Skye's pulse was already beginning to slow to a normal rate. "That's okay. I'm tired from the drive and I overreacted. What can I do for you?"

"I wanted to let you know what happened at the barbecue after you left."

Skye wasn't sure she wanted to know. But before she could say anything, Heather launched into the story of Clint's confrontation with Walt Harper.

"Dawn didn't hear all this, did she?"

"No, she had taken Mom to see her pony. But Mr. Slade, Dad and Beau heard."

It was late so they spoke only a few minutes more. Skye was smiling when she hung up the phone.

It pleased her that Clint had stood up for her. Despite his silence, maybe something she'd said this evening had meant something to him.

Don't get all happy and hopeful over this. He may not have been protecting your honor, he may just have been trying to protect his own privacy.

Dawn was out-of-sorts the next morning. Clint figured it was probably from all the excitement of the day before. He thought a ride on her pony might cheer her up, it usually did. But today, Princess seemed to sense Dawn's impatience, and while she was still settling herself into the saddle and trying to get her feet in the stirrups, Princess took off.

Dawn sat in the dust where she came to rest. Big tears rolled down her cheeks. "Princess dropped me."

Clint picked her up and cuddled her. Dawn cried, burying her face against his shoulder. He continued holding her, rubbing her back. Mixed with the gradually slowing sobs, he began to distinguish words.

"I want my mommy. I want my mommy."

Like a lightning bolt out of a clear blue sky, it hit him—he wanted her mommy, too!

Eleven

——

Despite Clint's assurances that Dawn was all right, Skye was worried. Why would he send his plane for her unless something was terribly wrong? Fortunately, the distance that took hours to travel by car was less than one by air.

Skye had never flown over this part of Texas before. Driving it, she knew there was a lot of wide-open ranch land, but from up above, she could see just how tiny the town of Harmony Ridge was in relation to surrounding ranches. Interstate 10 looked like a thin gray ribbon draped across the ground.

Reina opened the door when she reached the ranch. "They're in Dawn's room, Miss Skye."

She found Jack, Hope, Clint and Dawn together in the playroom.

"Mommy!" Dawn raced over to her.

Skye knelt to take her daughter in her arms. Dawn started to cry. Jack and Hope greeted Skye, then left the room. Clint stayed.

Skye wished he had left, as well. She was acutely aware of him watching her. Yesterday's encounter in his office was fresh and vivid in her memory.

Putting Clint from her mind, she focused on Dawn. "Hey, what's with all these crocodile tears, angel?"

"Princess dropped me."

Skye snuggled Dawn closer and looked toward Clint. "Is she okay?"

"I had Doc Beechem check her over. He said nothing's broken. That it probably scared her more than it hurt."

Dawn stiffened. Turning, she glared at Clint. "I was not scared." She looked at Skye, frowning. "Princess hurt my feelings, Mommy." She buried her face on her mother's shoulder.

Skye held her, rubbing her back and rocking gently. "Do you remember when you first asked about learning to ride and we talked about falling down?"

Dawn kept her head against Skye, nodding her agreement. "But I never *falled* before."

Skye understood what Dawn was feeling. First times for anything, bad or good, always had a bittersweet quality that intensified the emotions they evoked.

Dawn yawned. Gradually, she seemed to get heavier in Skye's arms, making her suspect at least part of the crankiness was caused by the need for a nap. Yesterday had been a big day for Dawn even though the little girl wasn't aware of all the emotional undercurrents surrounding the specifics of her birth.

As Skye continued comforting Dawn, she watched Clint, trying to see if all she'd told him yesterday had meant anything to him. If it did, nothing showed. Not in his body language, and not in his eyes.

She wanted to ask him about the incident with Walt. But from his cool demeanor, it seemed logical to assume he'd been protecting himself yesterday, not standing up for her.

She'd been foolish to even think he might have done it for her. He considered her "the queen of lies of omission" and had been completely straightforward about his never being able to forgive her for not telling him when she found out that she was pregnant. The sooner she accepted that fact, the better off she'd be.

When Skye was sure Dawn was fast asleep, she nodded her head toward the bedroom. Clint walked over to them and lifted Dawn from her arms. Skye sucked in her breath when in the process, the backside of his fingers skimmed her breasts.

"Sorry," he whispered.

But was he?

Skye followed as Clint carried Dawn into the bedroom and gently placed her on the bed.

They walked into the hallway.

"She didn't hit her head when she fell, did she?"

"No, she landed on her backside," he told her.

"Then it's all right for her to sleep."

"Actually, Doc Beechem recommended a nap." He gestured down the hallway. "Why don't we go into the family room?"

Skye agreed, grateful he hadn't suggested his office. Their next scheduled meeting with their attorneys was going to be awkward for her. She wondered if Clint would think about yesterday's incident at all. Of course it was possible she was only the latest in a long line of women he'd made love to in his office....

Once they were in the family room, Clint sat on the edge of the couch. He seemed tense and edgy.

Skye sat on the matching love seat. "Rough morning?"

"Dawn was a little cranky when she got up, but I figured she was extra tired from all the excitement yesterday."

"I'm sure she was."

"I thought a ride might cheer her up. But when she fell off her pony, she cried her little eyes out and kept asking for you."

Skye's heart went out to her daughter. She was torn between the need to always be there for her and her own need to avoid excessive contact with Clint. It was sheer torture being with him, knowing she loved him and knowing he would never return her feelings.

Yesterday, she'd poured out her heart to him and he hadn't seemed to care. He'd merely told her he'd send Reina back with Dawn and had let her go on her way.

Hopefully, she thought, the ache would lessen over time. At the moment, it was almost unbearable.

His edginess was wearing off on her, too. She felt angry at Clint for putting her in this position. If he wanted to share Dawn, he was going to have to learn to handle her in all her moods.

"It might have been better if you'd had Dawn talk to me on the phone," she told him.

"I asked and she just kept crying that she wanted you."

Be strong, Skye.

"Clint, we can't have her getting the idea that anytime she wants to see the one of us she's not with that it will be instantly arranged for her."

He frowned. "I didn't think you would mind coming."

Mentally she cringed, but stuck to her guns. "Of course I don't mind, but I want to be sure this doesn't become a habit."

"It won't." He shifted positions several times, as though he couldn't get comfortable. "Since you're here anyway, there are a few things I'd like to discuss."

She was planning on staying until after Dawn woke up, so time wasn't a problem. But she had been hoping Clint would have something else to do—maybe on the other side of the ranch. "All right."

Before Clint could begin, Hope walked into the room. "Where's Dawn?"

"She fell asleep, so I put her down for a nap," Skye answered.

"Bless her heart." Hope sat on the couch. "Would either of you like something to drink? Reina put some jars of sun tea out this morning, they should be ready about now.''

Skye shook her head. She also fought back a smile at Hope's offer. Even though her son was full-grown and this was his house now, complete with housekeeper, Hope automatically fell into the role of hostess.

Or was she playing mom?

It struck Skye that being a mother was more than eighteen years of commitment. It was a lifetime. A lifetime in which she would be in contact with Clint.

How many times in all those years to come would she fall into his arms, let him make love to her and then have him turn his back on her once his immediate needs were satisfied?

Probably as often as she let him get away with it.

Clint stood. ''No thanks, Mom. Skye and I were about to take a ride. Would you keep an eye out for Dawn until we get back?''

''Certainly.''

Was he trying to lure her off so they could be alone to make love?

Her self-respect demanded she not let it happen again. But her heart and her hormones urged her to settle for anything he was willing to give.

Time to get your act together, Skye.

''I don't know,'' Skye said. ''Maybe I should be here when she wakes up.''

''We won't be gone long,'' Clint assured her.

''I'll be sure she knows you're still at the ranch,'' Hope said.

Skye consented, but once they were on their way to the stables and out of earshot of anyone, she said, "As long as you realize that what happened yesterday isn't going to happen again."

"I want us away from the house so we can talk freely without anyone wandering in or overhearing us." He glanced her way. "As for the other, that's entirely up to you."

Somehow, that didn't soothe her qualms any.

With Clint on Zeus and Skye on the same chestnut mare she'd ridden the day Dawn had visited the Diamond S for the first time, they headed out to the nearest set of foothills. Clint led the way to a large oak tree halfway up one of the slopes.

After he helped her dismount, Skye moved away from him. Tilting one eyebrow, he questioned the abruptness of her escape. She didn't trust him to keep his hands to himself, and she didn't trust herself to make him stop if he started something.

"So what do you think of the view?" Clint asked.

She looked around. Nothing but wide-open spaces, lying beneath clear blue skies as far as the eye could see. Other than the land, scrubby vegetation and scattered oak trees were the only things there. Nothing man-made was in sight. "Its beautiful . . . very peaceful."

Clint took a deep breath and let it out slowly. "I've always thought so. You should see it after a good rain, lots of green grass and plenty of wildflowers. Sometimes this whole hill is covered in bluebonnets."

It sounded like the perfect place for a picnic. She could almost picture a patchwork quilt and overflowing picnic basket. Dawn would love picking wildflowers. Of course, if only she and Clint were sharing a picnic and the wildflowers, a whole new dimension could be added to the scene . . .

Keep daydreaming! That's a surefire way to be able to keep him at arm's length.

"Skye, about yesterday afternoon—"

"I told you, it's not going to happen again." She hated that desperate edge in her voice.

Clint held his palms out in surrender. "And I told you that it's entirely up to you."

Skye took a deep breath and let it out slowly.

Clint continued, "Before things got out of hand yesterday, I'd planned to tell you how well you'd handled yourself at the barbecue. It must have been a difficult situation for you, but you carried it off."

Skye was surprised by the compliment. "I did what I could. You were right when you said we needed to show a united front for Dawn."

"I'd also planned to tell you how proud I am of our daughter. You've done an excellent job raising her."

"I don't know what to say. Thank you, I guess."

He smiled at her. "You're welcome."

Skye caught herself before returning his smile, realizing his kind words had been chipping away at her defenses. If he reached for her, chances were she would end up in his arms.

Where was she going to find the willpower to resist him for years to come, when she couldn't even get through five minutes of conversation?

The cry of a hawk split the silence. Skye looked up, watching the bird soar.

"I haven't been to this particular spot for a long time," Clint said. "I was here the day I decided to buy a ring and ask Teresa to marry me."

She didn't want to hear this. In fact, if she never heard his ex-wife's name again it would be too soon.

"The peace and quiet helps clear my mind. The morning I woke up in my pickup at the Rocking W, I had the granddaddy of all hangovers. Spending half an hour up here did more for me than aspirin could have."

He must have awakened early that long-ago morning, because his truck had been gone when she'd looked out the window at six.

"I spent most of the time Teresa and I were dating trying to get her to have sex with me."

She *really* didn't want to hear this. "Clint, why are you telling me all this?"

"Yesterday you filled me in on some of what you went through six years ago. There are some things you should know from my side of what happened." He shoved his hands deep into his pockets. "You were right when you said I thought I was making love to Teresa that night."

Did he have any idea how hard it was for her to hear these things from him? "I already knew that."

"For what it's worth, I'm sorry."

She looked at him. His mouth was a tight, grim line.

"Clint, it happened a long time ago. I shouldn't even have bothered telling you."

"I'm glad you did. It put a lot of things in perspective. Your actions, my marriage and divorce."

Skye shrugged. She didn't want to hear about his marriage, or his divorce. He was Dawn's father, so yes their paths would cross. But she didn't have to care beyond their connection to Dawn.

At the moment, she was in love with him, but she would change that. She had no idea how, but certainly there had to be a way... there just had to be.

"You asked me once when I realized I wasn't in love with Teresa."

The night they'd been sitting on the swing, the reasons had seemed important. Now what difference would it make? Her silence was from indifference.

Clint must have assumed it was permission for him to continue. "It happened on our wedding night. I found out I'd never made love with Teresa."

"You fell out of love with your wife because she was a virgin? Most men would consider that a plus."

"I'm not explaining this very well." Clint settled his hat more firmly on his head and folded his arms across his chest. "Let's start way back at the beginning."

"Let's not," she said firmly. "I don't want to know about the two of you. I asked about it because I'd left Harmony Ridge so you two could be together and you ended up apart anyway. I was feeling cheated and wanted to know how it had happened. But it doesn't matter now."

"Please, hear me out."

"I don't see what good it will do."

"I let you have your say."

She wanted to say no, but he *had* let her have her say yesterday. She guessed she owed him the same courtesy. "All right."

"Growing up, I never had what I would call a friend. I knew plenty of people, but there wasn't anyone I could let my guard down with. At times I wanted that more than anything."

The switch in subject, from his relationship with Teresa, to himself, surprised Skye, almost as much as the information he'd shared with her.

"But you were student-body president and captain of the football team. You were voted most popular in your senior class."

"By acquaintances, not by friends," he said. "Don't get me wrong, I had a whole lot of good times in school and afterward, but it was all superficial connections. Anything deeper never happened. Except out here on the ranch. This spot and others . . . when I'm out here, something moves in my soul."

Skye looked at him. His eyes were barely visible in the shadow of his Stetson, so she sensed rather than saw his mixed emotions. She tried to steel herself against letting his revelations matter, but it was hard not to feel empathy. Clint must have had a lonely time of it growing up.

At least he'd had his connection with the land. Being here, seeing the beauty firsthand, she could understand how the land might affect him. "The view here *is* awe-inspiring."

"It's just one of many on the ranch. I ended up here by chance the day I decided to propose to Teresa. When I got here, I was fighting that hangover."

He'd mentioned a hangover earlier, but she'd thought he'd been talking about the morning after their encounter. Was this the same or a different hangover?

"Did you propose the same day you announced your engagement?"

"Yes."

The day after they'd made love!

"The day after you and I . . . ?"

He nodded slowly. "Until the night before I proposed to her, Teresa was just another female to me . . . one in a long line. I'd always figured sooner or later I'd settle down and get married, but at that point I had no plans of it being anywhere in the foreseeable future."

A cold shiver worked its way along her spine. Skye wanted to speculate, wanted to hope, but didn't dare. Instead, she asked Clint, "Why did you change your mind about getting married?"

"Because I was convinced I'd found the woman destined to be with me. I was no stranger to sex, and what I'd experienced the night before was so much more. Back then, all I identified was that it felt great, terrific, better than ever. Only later did I realize why. For the first time, someone had gotten through the barrier around me, and for a short time, the loneliness was gone."

Skye felt an urge to reach out to him, but held back.

"I figured I was set for life. But I was in for a rude awakening." Clint pushed his hat back and turned to face her. "When I found out Teresa was a virgin, I realized I hadn't been in love with her. How could I have fallen in love during something that clearly hadn't happened?"

"Didn't you ever wonder who you had made love to?"

"I'd been so drunk, I figured I must have dreamed that night in my pickup. Once I started having the dream again and again, that settled it in my mind. I was convinced my subconscious had created all those visions in my sleep, fulfilling my secret desire, giving me the experience of connecting completely with someone, finding a brief escape from the loneliness."

It was hard to imagine the smooth, cocky cowboy she'd admired from a distance had ever felt anything less than total self-confidence and satisfaction with his life.

"Having the dream repeat itself has been agony," he told her, "a constant reminder of what I thought I'd found, what I feared would never be mine." He moved until he was standing in front of her. "For years I've been kicking myself for making a wrong decision, for foolishly believing an alcohol-induced dream. But it wasn't the decision to get married that was wrong...the problem was, I had the wrong woman."

"The wrong woman?"

"All the tenderness and gentleness in the lovemaking you mentioned yesterday...it wasn't for Teresa. It was for you."

Skye was afraid to believe what her heart wanted so desperately to be true. "For me?" It was only two words, but her voice quivered trying to say them.

"Only for you."

She slipped her arms around his waist. He closed the embrace, gathering her against him.

He rested his cheek on top of her head. "I fell in love with you that night... tumbled head over heels."

She wasn't sure if she wanted to laugh or cry, so she simply snuggled closer to Clint.

He held her tighter. "I should have realized it as soon as you told me about Dawn. But I've been so busy learning to be a father, and so wrapped up in my anger at not knowing about her until now, that I missed the obvious—that you were the woman I'd fallen in love with, the woman I had decided to marry back then. Somewhere deep in my heart I knew. The dream started up again the night I stopped in at the Rocking W for coffee to go."

"I almost dropped a pitcher of iced tea when I turned around and saw you standing there."

He moved his hands in soothing circles on her back. "I didn't mean to scare you."

"I was afraid because of Dawn. And, I'd assumed you were still married. Oh, Clint..." She caught her bottom lip between her teeth. "I feel bad for Teresa. It wasn't her fault you didn't realize you'd made love to me instead of her."

"Our divorce had nothing to do with you. Even though I realized I hadn't fallen in love with Teresa, I tried my best to make my marriage work. But as it urned out, Teresa had only wanted me to add to the other ribbons and trophies in her collection. She also decided she liked city living and I wasn't about to leave the Diamond S for more than a few days at a time.''

She leaned against him, letting his words soak in, letting joy fill her heart. Until doubts started creeping in. "But can you forgive me for keeping Dawn a secret all these years?''

He tilted her chin up until she was looking at him. 'I'll always regret that things happened the way they did, but I can't blame you. I understand how you thought you were doing the right thing. You left for me. I didn't deserve such generosity then and I'm not sure I deserve it now.''

"But you missed all that time with Dawn. There's no way I can give it back to you.''

He rested one hand along each side of her face, caressing her skin with trembling fingertips. "What's killing me now is the thought of all those years I missed with you.''

He leaned forward and moved his mouth over hers. Skye sighed as she returned the kiss.

Clint ended the kiss slowly. "I realized something important while Dawn was crying for you this morning.'' He moved one hand to curve around the back of her head. "I'd woken up out-of-sorts myself, not sure why, but once she started up, I realized I wanted to throw a screaming hissy-fit, too. I wanted you here just as badly as she did, maybe more. I can't imagine going through the rest of my life without you . . . promise me I won't have to.''

"You won't."

"I love you, Skye."

"I love you, too."

He smiled. "Marry me?"

"Of course."

"As soon as possible?"

She had no doubts that he loved her and wanted to marry her, but she wondered if his wanting to marry as soon as possible had anything to do with Walt Harper's remarks yesterday. "You're not in a hurry because of what Walt said, are you?"

"How do you know about that?"

"Word travels fast."

"None of this has anything to do with Walt or whatever else anyone had to say on the matter. Like I told them last night, it's between you and me and isn't any of their business."

"It isn't any of their business or any of their *damned* business?" she teased.

He looked off to the side, then back to Skye. "Most likely the last one."

"You know everyone will probably have plenty to say about our getting married."

Clint nodded. "Don't be surprised if their first reaction is to say how nice it will be for Dawn."

"Oh, Clint, she'll be so excited."

"I'm sure she will, but I want you to know my love for you and my proposal has nothing to do with Dawn."

"Neither does my acceptance."

"Good. No matter what anyone else thinks, we both know Dawn is here because of what we have between us, not the other way around."

He kissed her, long, hard and deep. When he pulled back, Skye reached for his shirt buttons. "You wouldn't happen to have a blanket tucked in your saddlebags?"

"Hey, wait a minute." Clint laughed. "I thought you didn't come out here for that?"

Skye shrugged. "You said it was entirely up to me. So, do you have a blanket?"

"No, but you can bet I'll be keeping one in there from now on." She started to do up his buttons. He put his hand over hers. "Whoa, I said I didn't have a blanket, I didn't say you had to stop."

She looked skeptically at the brittle, brown grass. It would be a cushion against the hard ground beneath. But not enough of a cushion that she wanted to lie on it.

"The grass doesn't look all that comfortable this time of year."

Clint flashed her one of his sexy smiles. "Don't look so worried, darlin', I'll let you be on top."

*   *   *   *   *

TALLCHIEF'S BRIDE   Cait London

Man of the Month

The legend said that when a Tallchief placed the ring on the right woman's finger, he would capture true love. Talia Petrovna had gone to the ends of the earth to find Calum Tallchief's ring—but was a woman like her truly fated to be his bride?

A BRIDE FOR ABEL GREENE   Cindy Gerard

Northern Lights Brides

Mail-order bride Mackenzie Kincaid had prepared herself for a loveless marriage to Abel Greene. Now Abel was hesitant; he wanted out of the deal. If Mackenzie wanted to stay wedded, she *had* to seduce her husband!

LOVERS ONLY   Christine Pacheco

Workaholic Clay Landon was so caught up in securing the future that he'd neglected the present—and his wife, Catherine. Could Clay win her back and fulfil her dreams of raising his children?

ROXY AND THE RICH MAN   Elizabeth Bevarly

The Family McCormick

Wealthy businessman Spencer Melbourne hired private investigator Roxy Matheny to find his long-lost twin. Roxy knew she was in over her head— she could give him what he needed professionally, but what about more *personalized* services?

CITY GIRLS NEED NOT APPLY   Rita Rainville

Rugged single-father Mac Ryder knew that city girl Kathryn Wainwright wasn't prepared for the dangers of Wyoming. However, Kathryn knew that the confirmed bachelor was really the one in danger—of settling down with her!

REBEL'S SPIRIT   Susan Connell

Raleigh Hanlon hadn't seen the mischievous Rebecca Barnett in ten years, but now she was home again. Her zest for life had captivated him and he'd stopped even trying to keep her—and his imagination—under control!

COMING NEXT MONTH FROM

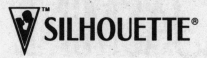 SILHOUETTE®

Sensation

*A thrilling mix of passion, adventure
and drama*

AT THE MIDNIGHT HOUR Alicia Scott
MUMMY'S HERO Audra Adams
MAN WITHOUT A MEMORY Maura Seger
MEGAN'S MATE Nora Roberts

Intrigue

Danger, deception and desire

GUARDED MOMENTS Cassie Miles
BULLETPROOF HEART Sheryl Lynn
EDGE OF ETERNITY Jasmine Cresswell
NO WAY OUT Tina Vasilos

Special Edition

Satisfying romances packed with emotion

MUM FOR HIRE Victoria Pade
THE FATHER NEXT DOOR Gina Wilkins
A RANCH FOR SARA Sherryl Woods
RUGRATS AND RAWHIDE Peggy Moreland
A FAMILY WEDDING Angela Benson
THE WEDDING GAMBLE Muriel Jensen

JASMINE CRESSWELL

Internationally-acclaimed Bestselling Author

SECRET SINS

The rich are different—they're deadly!

Judge Victor Rodier is a powerful and
dangerous man. At the age of twenty-seven,
Jessica Marie Pazmany is confronted with
terrifying evidence that her real name is
Liliana Rodier. A threat on her life prompts
Jessica to seek an appointment with her
father—a meeting she may live to regret.

**AVAILABLE IN PAPERBACK
FROM JULY 1997**

Bureau de Change

How would you like to win a year's supply of Silhouette® books? Well you can and they're FREE! Simply complete the competition below and send it to us by 31st January 1998. The first five correct entries picked after the closing date will each win a year's subscription to the Silhouette series of their choice. What could be easier?

1.	Lira	Sweden	____
2.	Franc	U.S.A.	____
3.	Krona	Sth. Africa	____
4.	Escudo	Spain	____
5.	Deutschmark	Austria	____
6.	Schilling	Greece	____
7.	Drachma	Japan	____
8.	Dollar	India	____
9.	Rand	Portugal	4
10.	Peseta	Germany	____
11.	Yen	France	____
12.	Rupee	Italy	____

C7G

Please turn over for details of how to enter...

How to enter...

It's that time of year again when most people like to pack their suitcases and head off on holiday to relax. That usually means a visit to the Bureau de Change... Overleaf there are twelve foreign countries and twelve currencies which belong to them but unfortunately they're all in a muddle! All you have to do is match each currency to its country by putting the number of the currency on the line beside the correct country. One of them is done for you! Don't forget to fill in your name and address in the space provided below and pop this page in a envelope (you don't even need a stamp) and post it today. Hurry competition ends 31st January 1998.

Silhouette Bureau de Change Competition
FREEPOST, Croydon, Surrey, CR9 3WZ
EIRE readers send competition to PO Box 4546, Dublin 24.

Please tick the series you would like to receive if you are a winner
Sensation™ ❏ Intrigue™ ❏ Desire™ ❏ Special Edition™ ❏

Are you a Reader Service™ Subscriber?   Yes ❏   No ❏

Ms/Mrs/Miss/Mr_____
                                          (BLOCK CAPS PLEASE)

Address_____

_____

_____ Postcode_____

(I am over 18 years of age)